This book belongs to

....

MERRY CHRISTMAS

LILY-MAY

200 Aesop's Fables

Compiled by Vic Parker

Miles Kelly

FROM
DAVE
&
GLORIA

2013

First published in 2012 by Miles Kelly Publishing Ltd
Harding's Barn, Bardfield End Green, Thaxted, Essex, CM6 3PX, UK

This edition printed 2013

2 4 6 8 10 9 7 5 3
•

Publishing Director Belinda Gallagher
Creative Director Jo Cowan
Editorial Director Rosie McGuire
Designer Joe Jones
Editorial Assistant Amy Johnson
Production Manager Elizabeth Collins
Reprographics Stephan Davis, Jennifer Hunt, Thom Allaway
Assets Lorraine King

ISBN 978-1-84810-659-8

Printed in China

British Library Cataloguing-in-Publication Data
A catalogue record for this book is available from the British Library

ACKNOWLEDGEMENTS
The publishers would like to thank the following artists who have contributed to this book:
Marco Furlotti, Jan Lewis
Advocate Art Natalie Hinrichsen, Tamsin Hinrichsen
Beehive Illustration Frank Endersby
The Bright Agency Marcin Piwowarski
Cover Tamsin Hinrichsen at Advocate Art

All other artwork from the Miles Kelly Artwork Bank

Made with paper from a sustainable forest

www.mileskelly.net   info@mileskelly.net

www.factsforprojects.com

Foreword

A fable is a short story that illustrates a life lesson, or moral. The fables in this book are believed to have been written by Aesop, a slave who lived in ancient Greece. Even though the stories are more than 2500 years old, their characters and humour are still relevant today.

Everyone enjoys cheering on the slow and steady tortoise as he overtakes the boastful hare, and no one can fail to laugh at the sneaky fox who gets his come uppance when served dinner by the stork!

The morals that accompany each fable can help to explain important lessons, such as those

learned by the
shepherd boy who
cried 'Wolf!' too many
times, and the country mouse
who realized his own little home was
a safe and happy place to live.

Aesop wrote more
than 580 fables. Within
the pages of this book
are 200 favourites,
which can be read and
enjoyed time and time again.

Contents

Funny Fates

Great and Small

Deadly Sins

Challenge and Chance

Schemes and Dreams

Mad Mistakes

Feathers and Fools

Heroes and Villains

The Key to Happiness

Narrow Escapes and Sticky Endings

Funny Fates

The Thirsty Pigeon

There was once a pigeon who had flown for many miles without water. She was desperate for a drink, but could not find a lake, a pond or even a puddle to sip from. Suddenly, she noticed a goblet of water painted on a signboard. The pigeon had no idea that it was only a picture, so she flew towards it excitedly. BANG! She crashed right into the signboard, then slid to the ground, her head spinning.

After that, the silly pigeon learnt to always take more care.

Enthusiasm should not outrun being cautious.

The Man
and the
Wooden God

Long, long ago in the early days of the world, people used to worship statues. They would pray to them for luck and good fortune, and give the statues offerings of food, wine and flowers to make them happy.

It so happened that there was a man who often prayed to a wooden statue that he had been given by his father. However, no matter how hard he prayed, and no matter what offerings he left, his luck never seemed to change nor his wishes be granted. He prayed and he prayed,

22

but still nothing ever changed.

One day, while the man was praying in front of the wooden god, he became frustrated and furious with its silence. In a temper, he went to the statue and with one blow swept it down from its pedestal. The statue broke in two, and gold coins streamed from inside it.

"Ah!" the delighted man cried. "You do have some use after all!"

Utility is most men's test of worth.

The Frog and the Ox

Once upon a time, a young frog was sitting with his father by the side of a pool. The pool was shady and cool, and the frogs were sitting happily among some rocks. They watched for passing flies, minding their own business and chatting to pass the time.

"Oh Father," said the little frog. "I have seen such a terrible monster! It was as big as a mountain, with horns on its head, and a long tail, and it had hoofs divided in two."

"Hush, child, hush," said the father frog,

"that was only Farmer White's ox. It isn't so big either — it may be a little bit taller than I, but I could easily make myself quite as broad, just you see." With that, the frog blew himself out, and blew himself out, and blew himself out.

"Was he as big as that?" he asked.

The young frog looked and thought for a second. "Oh, much bigger than that," he said, shrugging his shoulders.

Again the father frog blew himself out, and blew himself out, and blew himself out. Then he asked his son if the ox was as big as that.

The little frog looked and thought for a minute. "Bigger, Father, bigger," he replied, shaking his head.

So the father frog took a deep breath, and blew himself out, and blew himself out, and blew himself out... and he swelled and he swelled and

he swelled. And then he said,
"I'm sure the ox is not as big as..."
But at that very minute all the breath
whooshed out of him and he flew up and
away, zipping around like a balloon!

"Wow!" said the little frog.
"The ox was big, but he
couldn't do that."

Pride comes before a fall.

26

The Belly
and the
Members

There was once a body in which all the parts lived together in harmony. However, one day it occurred to the legs and arms that they were doing all the work and the belly was having all the food.

Now they had noticed this, they were not happy. So the parts of the body held a meeting, and decided to go on strike until the belly agreed to take its share of the work.

So for a day or two, the hands refused to take the food, the mouth refused to receive it, and the teeth had no work to do.

The members were pleased at first and felt sure that the belly would soon give in to their demands. But they began to find that they were not working well. The hands could hardly move, the mouth was parched and dry, while the legs were unable to support the body.

The members realized that the belly had been doing necessary work for them, even though they couldn't see it. They must all work together, or the body will grow sick.

It's important to work as part of a team.

The Fox and the Grapes

It was a hot summer's day, with a gentle breeze rustling the leaves of the trees and the bees buzzing lazily around the nodding flowers in the meadows.

A fox came strolling through an orchard, humming happily to himself, when he suddenly noticed a bunch of juicy grapes just ripening on a vine. The fox licked his lips. "Those delicious grapes would be just the thing to quench my thirst," he said to himself.

But the only problem was, he couldn't reach

them. The vine was hanging on a branch way up overhead.

Nevertheless, the fox was determined to have the grapes for himself. He stepped back several paces, took a run up and jumped as high as he could — he just missed.

"If at first you don't succeed, try, try, and try again," said the fox, turning round to try again. "One... two... three..." he counted and he was off — jumping up even higher than before. But again, the fox could not reach the grapes.

Again and again he tried to reach the tempting morsel, until he was even redder in the face than usual, and quite worn out. All the creatures in the orchard — from the worms to the bugs and the birds — were laughing.

At last, the fox had to admit defeat and he

gave up. As he walked away to the sound of
sniggering, he stuck his nose in the air and
said, "I am sure they are sour, anyway."

*It is easy to look down
on what you cannot get.*

The Man
and his
Wives

Long, long ago in the early days of the world, it was the custom for a man to have many wives. In these times, there was once a middle-aged man who had two wives — one wife that was old and one that was young.

Both wives loved the man very much. They each did everything they could to please him. So the man was very happy and they all lived together contentedly.

Now there came a time when the man's hair began to turn grey. The young wife did not like

this at all as she thought it made him look too old. She decided there was only one way to deal with this. Every night she took to combing his hair and picking out all the grey ones.

However, the older wife was pleased when she saw her husband going grey. This was because people had sometimes mistaken her for his mother! Every morning, she combed the man's hair and picked out the brown ones.

Of course, there was only one result – the man soon ended up entirely bald!

Give what you have to all and you will soon have nothing to give.

The Fox
and the
Mask

There was once a fox who got into the storeroom of a theatre. He strolled round, examining the scenery, costumes and props, wondering what everything was.

The fox was delighted when he came across what looked like a leg of chicken and a hunk of cheese, but when he bit into them – yuk! He found they were only made of paper and glue.

As he turned to see if he could find any real food, the fox saw a face glaring down at him. He sprang back in fear, but the face didn't move.

The fox became a little bolder and stopped shrinking back – still the face did not do so much as blink. Then the fox stepped closer – the face did not flinch. He stuck his tongue out and blew a raspberry. It was only a mask, the type actors use to put over their faces.

"Ah," said the fox, "you look very fine. It's a pity you don't have any brains."

Outside show is a poor substitute for inner worth.

Hercules
and the
Wagoneer

There was once a wagoneer who was driving a cart with a heavy load. It had been raining and the road was muddy. The horse heaved the cart along, and the wagoneer guided him onto the firmest parts of the road.

Despite this, the wheels sank in the mud. The wagoneer set his shoulder to the cart and urged the horse forwards, but the more they

heaved, the deeper the wheels sank.

So the wagoneer prayed to the ancient hero Hercules, who was famous for his great strength.

"Hercules, please help me!" he cried.

"You called?" came a booming voice.

The wagoneer spun round to see a giant of a man, with a lion skin wrapped round his shoulders. Hercules — for it was he — said, "Don't just stand there. I'm not going to do it for you! Set your shoulder to the wheel for one more push, and this time I'll help."

Fate helps those who help themselves.

The Man
and the
Satyr

Long, long ago, creatures called satyrs, which were half-man, half-goat, lived alongside humans.

One bitterly cold winter's night, a man had lost his way in a deep, dark wood. As he was trying to find his way home, he stumbled across a satyr who was gathering firewood. The satyr was kind and helpful. As soon as he discovered that the man had lost his way, he asked him back to his own house.

"You can stay with me for the

night," the satyr offered. "I will guide you out of the forest in the morning."

The man gratefully accepted the satyr's offer and went along with him to his little wooden hut. As they walked through the forest, the satyr noticed that the man kept raising his hands to his mouth and blowing on them. "I hope you don't mind me asking, but why do you keep doing that?" asked the satyr.

"My hands are numb with the cold," said the man, "and my hot breath warms them up."

"I see," said the satyr

thoughtfully, and continued leading the way to his home.

The little wooden hut wasn't much further on, which the man was very glad to see. Soon the pair were both inside in the warm, and the satyr put a steaming bowl of porridge before the man, who happily picked up a spoon to eat. But when he raised the spoon to his mouth, he began blowing upon it.

The satyr looked puzzled. "May I ask why you are doing that?" he said.

"Well, the porridge is too hot, and my breath will cool it," explained the man.

To the man's great surprise, the satyr suddenly stood up, opened the door, and bundled him out into the cold and dark.

"Out you go," said the satyr. "I'm not sure what you are, but I will have nothing to do with

you. If you can blow hot and cold with the same breath, you must be dangerous."

"But... but... but..." the man tried to explain, but he was talking to the door.

Never trust a changeable person.

The Horse and his Rider

There was once a young man who fancied himself to be a good rider. One market day, he saw a fine-looking horse for sale and was determined to ride it. He did not know that the horse had not been properly broken in, and he didn't think to ask. He just climbed a nearby fence and dropped onto the horse's back, regardless.

The second the horse felt a rider's weight in the saddle, it set off at full gallop, with the young man hanging on for dear life.

One of the rider's friends saw him thundering down the road. Surprised, he called out, "Where are you off to in such a hurry?"

Gasping for breath, the young man pointed to the stallion, and replied, "I have no idea – you will have to ask the horse."

Act in haste and you will have to go along with the consequences.

The Two Crabs

There was once a mother crab and her child, who lived on the seabed. The mother crab took great care to teach the little crab good manners and behaviour.

One day, the mother crab said that she would take her little one up to the seashore as a treat. "But you must be on your best behaviour," she said. "I don't want all the land creatures thinking that we

44

sea creatures are common."

"I will try, Mother," promised the little crab.

So up, up, up they went, until they reached the sandy shore. Once there, they decided to go for a stroll.

They hadn't gone far when the mother crab hissed at her child, "You are walking ungracefully. You should try to walk forwards without twisting from side to side."

"I will try," said the young crab. "Please show me how and I will follow you."

It is best to lead by example.

The Man, the Boy and the Donkey

There was once a man and his son who were on their way to market with their donkey. They walked along the road, leading the donkey behind them, minding their own business. After a while a countryman passed by them and shouted out, "You fools, what is a donkey for but to ride upon?"

The man looked at the boy, and the boy looked at the man, and they both said, "Why, he is right!" So the man put his son on the donkey and they went on their way.

A little while later they passed a group of
men and they heard one of them say, "Look at
that lazy youngster! He allows his poor father to
walk in this heat, while he rides on the donkey.
Shame on him!"

The man looked at the boy, and the boy
looked at the man, and they both said, "Why, he
is right!" So the man ordered his son to climb
down, and he got on the donkey himself.

They hadn't travelled much further when
they passed two women. One woman pointed at
the man on the donkey and shouted, "Shame on
that lazy lout, making his poor little son trudge
along while he rides on the donkey."

The man looked at the boy, and the boy
looked at the man, and they both felt rather
confused by this. The man thought for a while,
uncertain of what to do next. Eventually, he

pulled his son up before him on the donkey so they could both travel in comfort, and they carried on with their journey.

By this time they had come to the town, and passersby began to jeer and point at them. The man stopped and asked what they were pointing at. One man said, "Aren't you ashamed of yourself for overloading that poor donkey?"

FUNNY FATES

The man looked at the boy, and the boy looked at the man, and they both got off the donkey at once. They stood wondering what to do. They thought and thought, until at last they took a pole, tied the donkey's feet to it, and raised the pole and the donkey to their shoulders. They went along amid the laughter of all who met them until they came to a bridge. Then the donkey, getting one of its feet loose, kicked out and broke free. Off it ran, never to be seen again by the man or his son.

"That will teach you," said an old man who had followed them along the way. "You can't please everybody."

Please all, and you will please none.

The Mule's Brains

There was once a time when the lion and the fox went hunting together. The fox thought up a cunning plan to catch a mule. So the lion, playing his part, sent a message to the mule inviting him to meet, to talk about their two families going into partnership. Of course the mule was delighted at this, and he went to see the lion at once. But when he arrived, the lion simply pounced on him and killed him with one blow of his mighty paw.

Then the lion yawned lazily and said to the

fox, "Here is our dinner. You watch it while I go and nap. Don't dare eat any of it, mind."

The lion went off for a nap and the fox waited... and waited... and waited. After a long time, there was still no sign of the lion. So the fox took the mule's brains and ate them up.

Not long afterwards, the lion returned. At once he gave a terrible roar and demanded, "Fox! What have you done with the brains?"

"Brains?" the fox replied. "It had none, or it would never have fallen into your trap."

Wit always has an answer ready.

The Gnat and the Bull

There was once a huge bull who spent his days grazing in a field. One day, a tiny gnat came along and landed on one of the bull's horns for a rest.

The gnat found the place to his liking, and remained sitting there for a long time. He was quite nervous, for he knew that if he bothered the bull, the massive creature could kill him with a flick of his tail. However, as the bull had not said anything, he decided to boldly stay as long as he could.

FUNNY FATES

Finally, the gnat had rested enough and was about to fly away, when he politely asked the bull, "Do you mind if I go now?"

The bull merely raised his eyes and said without interest, "It makes no difference to me. I didn't notice when you arrived, and I won't know when you leave."

We may be more important in our own eyes than in the eyes of others.

The Boasting Traveller

There was once a man who travelled the world. He went near and far, here and there, seeing all sorts of wonderful sights and having all kinds of fabulous adventures.

Then came the time for him to return home. He arrived back with incredible tales of all the amazing things he had seen and done in foreign countries. At first, his friends listened to the man with great interest. But as he went on and on, they grew bored with his tales – and began to wonder if he was even telling the truth.

One thing the man boasted about most was a jumping competition he had entered in Rhodes. He claimed that he had completed a long jump that no one could beat.

"Just go to Rhodes and ask the people there," he said. "Everyone will tell you it's true."

But the man's friends said, "If you can jump as far as that, we needn't go there to prove it. Let's imagine this is Rhodes — jump now!"

Actions speak louder than words.

The Lion, the Mouse and the Fox

A **lion was once asleep** when a mouse ran over his back. The mouse's feet tickled the lion and he woke with a start. He had no idea why he had been so suddenly awoken, and looked around to see what had disturbed him.

A fox lurking nearby had seen this happen, and he

thought it would be great fun to have a joke at the lion's expense.

"This is the first time I've seen a lion afraid of a mouse," said the fox loudly.

The lion was embarrassed, but tried to pretend he wasn't. "Afraid of a mouse?" he said. "Not I! It's his bad manners I can't stand."

If you take a small liberty with someone, it might cause great offence.

The Fawn and his Mother

There was once a hind who had a baby fawn. She cared for him well, and the fawn grew to be big and strong.

However he seemed to be afraid of everything. He would jump at the slightest rustle of a bush, and start at the smallest snap of a twig. If he ever heard the barking of a dog – even in the distance – he

would be off as fast as his legs could carry him.

One day, the mother hind looked at her son and said, "My boy, nature has given you a powerful body and a stout pair of antlers. You could charge at anything with those and run them right through! I can't think why you are such a coward as to run away from everything."

Just then they both heard the sound of a pack of hounds in full cry – they knew that huntsmen must be coming.

"You stay where you are," said the hind. "Don't worry about me!" And with that, she ran off as fast as her legs could carry her.

No arguments will give courage to the coward.

The Prophet

Long, long ago there were people to whom, it was believed, the gods revealed what would happen in the future. These people were called prophets.

There was once a prophet who sat in the market-place and told the fortunes of anyone who cared to ask. People loved to hear what was going to happen to them – even if it was bad news – so he was kept busy every day.

One morning, the prophet was in the middle of telling the fortunes of a huge queue of people

when a boy suddenly pushed through the crowds. The boy told the prophet that his house had been broken into by thieves, and that they had made off with everything they could lay their hands on.

The prophet jumped to his feet and rushed off, cursing the thieves. Bystanders were amused, and one said, "Our friend claims to know what is going to happen to others, but he's not clever enough to see what's in store for himself."

Only follow those who lead by example, not by empty words.

The Bald Huntsman

There was once a man who had a fine head of hair. However, as he grew old it began to fall out, and he ended up entirely bald.

The man didn't like being bald and worried that people might think he looked better before. So he had a wig made, which was just like his own hairstyle, so the man thought no one would notice.

One day, the man went hunting with friends. He was wearing his wig as usual, with his hat perched on top. It was a windy day, so the man didn't get very far before a particularly big gust of wind caught his hat and carried it off – with his wig too. How all the other huntsmen laughed!

The man had a good sense of humour. He entered into the joke, and said, "If the hair that wig is made of didn't stick to the head on which it grew, no wonder it won't stick to mine."

Laugh and the world laughs with you.

The Oxen
and the
Axletrees

Once upon a time, a pair of oxen were drawing a heavily loaded wagon along the highway. As they tugged and strained, a part of the wagon called the axletrees began to creak and groan with the strain. The more the oxen heaved and pulled, the more the

66

axletrees squealed and moaned.

This annoyed the oxen dreadfully. Finally, the temper of one snapped. With a great bellow, he turned round and looked back at the wagon, shouting, "Hey, you there! Why do you make such a noise when we do all the work?"

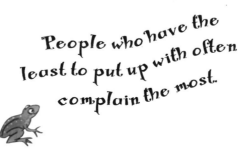

People who have the least to put up with often complain the most.

Great
and Small

The Mountains in Turmoil

Once upon a time, a group of villagers built their homes around the base of some towering mountains.

The mountains were like giants — huge and threatening — but the villagers didn't want to move anywhere else because the earth around the mountains was rich, and crops grew well.

One day, smoke started to pour from the mountain tops, the earth began to quake and rocks came tumbling down. The people were terrified that the mountains had come to life.

70

They felt sure that something awful was happening. Everyone huddled together, convinced they were going to die.

Suddenly the earth shook violently and a huge gap appeared in the side of the mountains. The people fell to their knees and waited for the end to come.

At long last, a teeny tiny mouse poked its head and whiskers out of the gap and came scampering towards them.

And that was the end of it!

There is often much fuss about nothing.

71

The Mice
and the
Weasels

The mice and the weasels were sworn enemies, and there came a time when things got so bad that they went to war. They fought battle after battle, but the mice always came off the worst, with many being killed and eaten by the weasels.

At last the mice realized that they were near to being defeated once and for all. So they called a meeting to discuss if there was anything they could do that they had not already thought of, to avoid disaster. All of the oldest,

wisest mice were there, solemnly putting their heads together to try to think of plans. Then one old mouse got up to speak.

"It's no wonder we are always beaten, for we have no generals to plan our battles and direct the movements of our troops in the field."

This made a lot of sense to the other mice and they acted on his advice. They at once chose the biggest mice to be their generals. These mice, in order to be marked out as different from the foot soldiers, wore big helmets decorated with plumes of straw. The generals then led the mice to battle, confident of victory... however, they were defeated as usual.

Soon, all the mice were scampering as fast as they could back to their holes. They all made their way to safety without difficulty, except the generals. They couldn't squeeze into their holes

because their helmets were too broad
and the plumes of straw on top were
too tall. So they were left to the clutches
of the weasels.

Greatness carries its own
dangers and punishments.

74

The Wolf and the Kid

Goats are very good at scrambling up and down steep mountainsides, climbing where others can't go.

Once upon a time, a kid clambered on top of a store shed in the farmyard and perched on the roof, looking down proudly on everyone below. Just then, a wolf slunk by, casting his eyes around greedily for a possible meal. Immediately, the kid began to tease and taunt the wolf – for he felt quite safe up on the roof.

"Mr Wolf," he cried. "You are a murderer and a

thief. I don't know how you dare show your face near the homes of honest folk. We know the crimes you commit!"

"Curse away, my young friend," said the wolf. "You are only being so bold because you know that I can't get my claws into you at the moment."

It is easy to be brave when you are a safe distance from danger.

The Fox
and the
Lion

There was once a fox who was happy living in the woods, where he knew and was at peace with his neighbours. However one day, a lion prowled into the neighbourhood. When the fox first saw the lion he was terribly frightened, and ran away to hide.

It wasn't long before the fox crossed the lion's path again. However this time, he didn't run away. Instead he stopped at a safe distance from the King of the Beasts and watched as he passed by.

Soon afterwards, the fox found himself in the

same part of the woods as the lion yet again. This time, the fox wasn't taken by surprise by the mighty creature. He had quite lost his fear.

The fox went straight up to the lion, passing the time of day with him, asking how his family was faring and when he might have the pleasure of seeing him again. Then, turning on his tail, the fox parted from the lion — he didn't run, but just strolled casually away.

Familiarity breeds contempt.

The Bald Man
and the Fly

It was a hot summer's day and a bald man
who had finished work sat down under a
shady tree to rest. How pleasant it was,
relaxing in the cool. His eyelids began to
droop and his head started to nod.

Just as the man was about to fall
asleep, a fly began hovering round his
head. Buzz! Buzz! Buzz! The man was
very annoyed. Buzz! Buzz! Buzz! The
fly zipped this way and that, darting
forwards and stinging him here and there.

The bald man was hugely annoyed and began swatting at his enemy, aiming blow after blow at the buzzing creature. But again and again he missed, and his hand landed on his own head instead! Still the fly tormented him.

Finally the man gave up, allowing the fly to buzz where it liked. "I will hurt myself more than it is hurting me, if I carry on," he said to himself.

If you seek to harm an enemy, you may only end up hurting yourself.

The Lion
and the
Statue

Once upon a time, a man and a lion were unlikely travelling companions on a long journey. They chatted as they went, and in the course of conversation they began to boast about how strong and bold they were, each claiming to be more courageous than the other.

"Me and my family have killed an elephant, largest of all beasts," bragged the lion.

"But I have slain a mighty stag singlehandedly," returned the man.

And so they went on, squabbling all the

way, until they came to a crossroads where there was a statue of a man overpowering a lion.

"There!" said the man triumphantly. "Look at that. Doesn't that prove that men are stronger than lions?"

"Not so fast, my friend," said the lion, "that is only your view of the contest. If lions could make statues, you may be sure that you would see the man underneath."

There are two sides to every story.

83

Hercules and Minerva

In ancient days long gone by, Hercules was a hero – half-man, half-god, and known all over the world for feats of incredible strength. Minerva was one of the goddesses who ruled on Mount Olympus, famous for being very wise.

One day, Hercules was travelling along a narrow road when he saw on the ground in front of him what appeared to be an apple. As he passed, he stamped on it with his heel. To his astonishment, instead of being crushed, it doubled in size. That made Hercules even more determined to squash it. He got out his mighty club and gave the apple as good a bash as he could. However the apple just swelled to an enormous size and blocked the road. Hercules dropped his club and stood staring in shock.

Just then Minerva appeared, and said to Hercules, "Leave it alone, my friend. That which you see is the apple of discontent. If you do not meddle with it, it remains small as it was, but if you rouse it, the apple swells into the monstrous thing that you see before you."

It is sometimes better to walk away from an argument and forget it than try to tackle it.

The Ants

Long ago, ants were once people and made their living by farming the land. However, people weren't content with the results of their own hard work. They were always looking longingly at their neighbours' crops, which seemed much better than their own. Whenever they could lay their hands on their neighbours' produce, they stole it, and hid it in their store houses.

In those days, the gods and goddesses of Mount Olympus ruled the world.

When father of the gods, Jupiter, saw how things had become, he was disgusted with humankind. He was so furious that he changed people into ants.

However, although their bodies changed, their nature remained the same. So to this day, people go about the cornfields and gather the fruits of others' labours, and store them up for their own use.

You may punish a thief, but he will always remain a thief.

The Fisherman Piping

One day a fisherman had a new idea for how he might catch fish. He thought that if he took his flute to the riverbank and played a jolly tune, the fish might hear the music, and come to the surface and dance – making it easy for the fisherman to catch them.

So he began to play one merry tune after another, but not a single fish put so much as its nose out of the water. The fisherman gave up, laid down his flute, and went back to his old method of just casting his net into the water.

To his astonishment, when he drew the net in it was heavy with fish! Then the fisherman took up his flute and played again, and as he played, the fish flipped and flapped in the net.

"Ah, you dance now when I play," said he.

"Yes," replied an old fish, "now we have no choice."

When you are in a person's power you must do as they bid.

The Bee and Jupiter

Long, long ago, when the world was very young, great gods and goddesses ruled the Earth from their home on Mount Olympus.

One day, a queen bee flew up to Olympus with some fresh honey from her hive. It was a present for the king of the gods, Jupiter.

Jupiter was highly pleased with the bee's thoughtful gift. In return, he promised to give the delighted queen bee anything she liked.

The insect thought hard — she did not want to waste such a wonderful reward. Finally, she

announced that she would
be grateful to Jupiter if he
would give stings to her
and all her kind. Jupiter
was taken aback by
this, and asked why. The
queen explained that it would
allow them to sting people who stole their honey.
Jupiter wasn't happy about this, for he loved
humankind, but he had given his word. So he
agreed. Yet the stings he gave were of such a
kind that whenever a bee stings someone, the
sting is left in the wound and the bee dies.

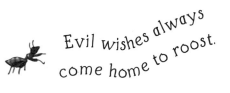

Evil wishes always
come home to roost.

The Fir Tree and the Bramble

There was once a forest in which lived a very proud fir tree. She thought she was better than all the other trees, bushes and plants because she grew taller and straighter than anything else she could see.

One day she began boasting to a bramble, and said in a very snooty manner, "You poor thing, you are of no use whatsoever. Now, look at me – I am useful for lots of things. For instance, when people build houses, they always choose fir. They can't do without me."

The bramble wasn't upset at all. She cleverly replied, "Ah, that's all very well, but you wait until people come with axes to cut you down. Then you'll wish you were a bramble and not a fir."

It is sometimes better to be poor without any cares, than to be rich and weighed down with duties.

The Lion
and the
Wild Ass

A lion and a wild ass once struck up an unlikely partnership – they decided to go hunting together.

The plan was that the wild ass, who could run very fast and had great strength and stamina, was to run down whichever animal they had decided upon. Then when the animal was worn out, the lion would pounce and swiftly kill it with his ferocious jaws and razor-sharp claws.

Strange though the plan might seem, it worked well. The two animals had success after success. However, when it was time to share the spoils, the lion divided everything into three, not two, equal portions.

"I will take the first," he said, "because I am King of the Beasts. I will also take the second, because, as your partner, I am entitled to half of what remains. As for the third — well, unless you give it to me and take yourself off pretty quick, the third, believe me, will make you feel very sorry for yourself!"

Might makes right.

The Fisher
and the
Little Fish

A fisher had once been fishing all day long and had caught nothing at all. Evening was about to draw in, but there was just time for the fisher to cast his nets one last time before going home.

When he drew the nets in, he saw that he had caught something at last. However, it was just a single little fish, which looked up at him and begged for mercy.

"Pray, let me go, master," said the fish. "I am much too small for you to eat just now. Look at me – I am hardly going to make a bite, let alone a whole meal. If you put me back into the river, I shall soon grow much bigger, then you can make a splendid banquet of me."

But the fisher shook his head. "No no, my little fish," he said. "I am very lucky to have you now. Another time, I may not get you at all."

A little thing in the hand is worth more than a great thing that you do not have yet.

The Fly
and the
Mule

Once upon a time, a mule was plodding slowly down a road, pulling a cart. A tiny fly suddenly appeared and sat on the edge of the cart.

"How slow you are!" said the fly. "Can't you go faster? I'm in a hurry! Speed up or I will use my sting as a whip."

However the mule was not in the least bit bothered. "Behind me in the cart," he said, "sits my master. He holds the reins and flicks me with his whip, and I obey him. I'm not going to take any notice of your cheek. I know when I have to go fast and when it's better to go slow."

Life is not just about going at top speed.

The Mouse and the Bull

There was once a bull who was feeding on a bale of straw. He had no idea that a mouse was living there. The mouse was angry that the bull was about to destroy his home. As the bull lowered his head to eat, the tiny mouse bit the great animal on the nose. Cheekily, the mouse then disappeared into a hole in the wall.

Despite the surprise, the bull charged at the wall, butting it with his huge head – but the wall held firm. After a while, the bull became tired and sank to the ground. Then, when all was quiet, the mouse ran out and bit him again!

 The bull was beside himself. He rose to his feet, but the mouse ran back in the hole again, and the bull could do nothing but bellow and fume. Then he heard a shrill voice say, "You big fellows don't always have it your way – sometimes we little ones come off best."

The battle is not always won by the strong.

The Lion
and the
Mouse

Once, a little mouse came upon a lion who was fast asleep. The mouse had never seen a lion close up before and was very curious to see what his great mane felt like. Very boldly, the mouse crept as nimbly as he could up the lion's leg, along his back, and all the way to his soft, thick mane. However, even though the mouse was being as light and quiet as he could, his movements woke the mighty beast.

As the mouse ran back down the lion's leg, an enormous paw clamped down upon his tail. Then the lion snarled and opened his big jaws to swallow him.

"Pardon, oh King," cried the little mouse, trembling in terror. "Forgive me this time, and I shall never forget it. You never know, I may even be able to return the favour one of these days."

At this bold idea, the lion began to laugh. He was so amused at the thought of the mouse being able to help him that he let him go.

Some time after, the lion was unlucky enough to be caught in a trap. The rejoicing hunters wanted to carry their prize alive to show their king. So they bound the injured lion and tethered him to a tree while they went in search of a wagon to carry him on.

Just then, the little mouse happened to pass by, and recognized the lion at once. Seeing his sad plight, the mouse scampered straight up to him. It was only a few moments before he had gnawed away the ropes and the lion was free.

"You see?" said the little mouse. "Was I not right after all?"

Little friends may prove great friends.

The Eagle
and the
Beetle

Long ago, an eagle was chasing a hare, who was running for her life. She was at her wits end to know where to turn for help.

At last the hare saw a beetle and begged him to help her. Although the beetle was tiny, he swore he would do what he could to help.

The hare sank down exhausted, and the eagle swooped in for the kill. But the tiny beetle puffed up his chest and stood tall. He shouted to the eagle not to touch the hare, for she was under his protection. Of course the eagle never noticed the beetle – he was far too small. So the bird just seized the hare and ate her up.

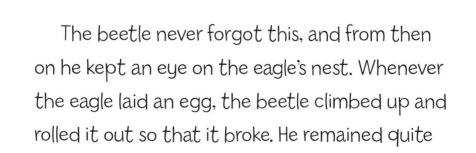

The beetle never forgot this, and from then on he kept an eye on the eagle's nest. Whenever the eagle laid an egg, the beetle climbed up and rolled it out so that it broke. He remained quite

unseen by the eagle, who became desperate at the loss of all her eggs.

At last the eagle grew so worried over the loss of her eggs that she went to the great god Jupiter, who was the special protector of eagles.

"Please help me great Jupiter," begged the eagle. "I cannot bear to keep losing my eggs this way. I need a safe place in which to keep them."

The god took pity on the eagle and invited her to lay her eggs in his lap. There he could keep a close eye on them.

The beetle had been watching and listening to the eagle's pleas. Immediately, he made a ball of dirt the size of an eagle's egg, and flew up and placed it in Jupiter's lap. When Jupiter saw the dirt, he stood up to shake it out of his robe, and, forgetting about the eagle's eggs, he shook them out too.

The eggs were broken just as before. And ever since then, eagles never lay their eggs in the season when beetles are out and about.

The weak can always find ways to avenge an insult, even upon the strong.

The Lion, Jupiter and the Elephant

The lion, for all his size and strength, and his sharp teeth and claws, is a coward in one way – he can't bear the sound of a cockerel crowing, and he runs away whenever he hears it.

Once, the lion complained bitterly to the great god Jupiter for making him like that, but Jupiter said it wasn't his fault and he had done the best he could for him. Jupiter also said that, considering this was the lion's only weakness, he ought to be content.

The lion, however, wouldn't be comforted, and

was so ashamed of his timidity that he prowled around with a heavy heart.

One day the lion met the elephant and the two got talking in friendly conversation. The lion noticed that the great beast cocked up his ears all the time, as if he were listening for something, and the lion couldn't resist asking why he did so. Just then a tiny gnat came humming by, and the elephant said, "Do you see that wretched little buzzing insect? I'm terribly afraid that it

will get into my ear — if it gets in, I'm done for. That's why I keep flapping my ears — to keep the little gnat out of them."

The lion's spirits rose at once when he heard this. "For," he said to himself, "if the elephant, huge as he is, is afraid of a gnat, I needn't be so much ashamed of being afraid of a cockerel, which is ten thousand times bigger than a gnat."

There is no shame in being afraid, no matter how big you are.

The Gnat
and the
Lion

There was once a tiny gnat who had no fear. He went striding up to a lion, who could barely see him, and said, "I am not in the least bit afraid of you. What does your strength amount to after all? I'm stronger than you. If you don't believe it, let us fight and see." With that, the gnat sounded his battle horn, darted in and bit the lion's nose.

When the lion felt the sting, he was furious. However in his haste to swat the gnat, he only succeeded in scratching his nose and making it bleed. He failed altogether to hurt the gnat, which buzzed off in triumph, overjoyed.

The gnat's celebrations were short-lived however. It flew straight into a spider's web, and was caught and eaten by the spider. And so the gnat fell prey to an insignificant creature after having triumphed over the King of the Beasts.

No one is so great that they cannot fail.

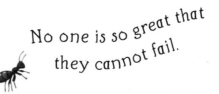

The Tree
and the
Reed

There was once a tree that had been
planted years ago and had grown
enormously, towering over other nearby trees.
At its foot grew a reed, slender and delicate.

The two often talked to each other, and one
day the tree said, "Well, little one, why don't
you ever grow taller? Just plant your feet deeply
in the ground and raise your head more boldly in
the air as I do."

"I am very content with my lot," said the reed.
"I may not be grand, but I think I am safer."

"Safe!" sneered the tree. "Look at me – no one would be able to pluck me up by the roots, but they could easily do that to you!"

Soon after, the tree had reason to regret its words. A hurricane tore it down, reducing it to little more than a pile of logs and branches. But the little reed was able to bend before the force of the wind. And as soon as the storm was over, it stood straight up again.

Obscurity often brings safety.

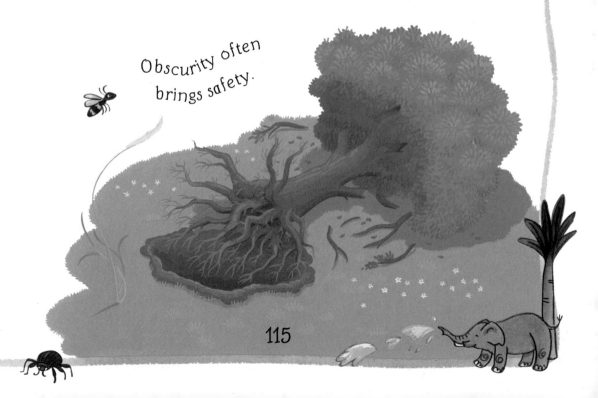

115

Deadly Sins

The Thrush
and the
Fowler

A thrush once spied a myrtle bush covered in bright, juicy berries. She flew down and began to eat, hardly able to believe her luck. The little bird ate berry after berry until she was quite full. She couldn't stop because the berries were delicious!

The thrush was so busy plucking off the berries that she didn't notice a bird-catcher, or fowler, approach. He spotted the plump little bird at once and his eyes sparkled. Quickly and quietly, he took out some long reeds he had brought and spread them with sticky bird lime. Then, still unnoticed, he poked the reeds into the myrtle bush.

Of course, it wasn't long before the thrush hopped onto one of the reeds and she was caught fast. Knowing she was about to be killed, the thrush cried, "How foolish I am! For the sake of a little pleasant food I have given up my life."

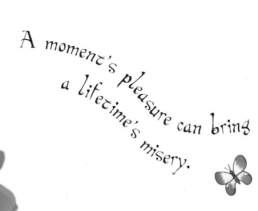

A moment's pleasure can bring a lifetime's misery.

The Old Woman and the Wine Jar

There was once an old woman who lived a simple life. She worked hard to make sure that she had a roof over her head and food on the table, and every now and again she had a little money left over to treat herself to a glass of wine. How she would enjoy sitting and savouring her little luxury, relishing every drop.

There came a time when the old woman had not been able to afford any wine for several weeks. One day she was travelling along the road when she noticed a wine jar lying in the grass.

Even though she knew it would almost certainly be empty, she had to make sure.

When the old woman picked up the wine jar she found that yes, it was drained to the dregs. However, she couldn't resist holding it to her nose and taking a sniff at the mouth of the jar.

"Ah," she cried, "what memories cling around the things that give us pleasure!"

It is hard to break the habit of a lifetime.

The Serpent and the File

One hot day, a snake was slithering along, going nowhere in particular, when it glided into the workshop of a craftsman who made armour. The workshop was cool and shady and the snake slid further in, looking for a safe corner in which to curl up and rest.

As it slithered over the floor, it suddenly felt its skin scratched by a rough tool called a file, which the workman had left lying on the ground. In a rage, the snake turned on it and tried to pierce the iron file with its fangs – but all it succeeded in doing was hurting its mouth.

It is a waste of time to get angry about unfeeling things.

The Two Neighbours

Long, long ago, in the early days of the world, two neighbours prayed to the great god Zeus, who ruled over the Earth. The neighbours presented gifts and bowed low to the ground. Then they begged Zeus, who was all-knowing and all-powerful, to grant them their hearts' desires.

Zeus looked deep inside them and saw that one of the neighbours burned with a terrible greed for money, or avarice, which could never be fulfilled. And Zeus saw that the heart of the other neighbour was on fire with envy. So to teach them both a lesson, the wise god decided that he would grant each man whatever he wished for himself, but on one condition – the other neighbour would get twice as much.

After the two neighbours had prayed, they began to wish for their hearts' desires, to see if Zeus had heard and answered them.

The first neighbour shut himself inside his house and wished for a room filled with gold. Imagine his astonishment when it appeared before him! But his delight was short-lived, for a few minutes later his neighbour came running to his door to tell him that two rooms of gold had appeared in his house.

Of course, this man quickly became unhappy too. Instead of being pleased that he had double the treasure, he was envious that his neighbour had been answered by Zeus and had any treasure at all. He instantly found himself wishing that his greedy neighbour might lose one of his eyes. Of course, it was no sooner said than done – but he himself lost both, and became totally blind.

Vices are their own punishment.

The Hare
and the
Tortoise

A hare was once *boasting* to the other animals about how speedy he was.

"No one is faster than me," he said with a smirk. "I challenge anyone to prove me wrong – who is bold enough to race with me?"

Of course, no one dared put themselves forward, until a tortoise slowly lifted his head and spoke. "I accept your challenge," the old, wrinkled one announced softly.

The hare burst out laughing. "Oh, that is funny, please tell me you are joking."

But the tortoise was deadly serious. "Save your boasting until you've beaten me," he said.

The other animals, astonished, rushed to set a course. It took the tortoise several minutes to amble to the start line. Some of the animals muttered to each other and shook their heads.

"Ready, set, go!" bellowed the ox – and finally the race began.

The hare darted out of sight. But as soon as he had rounded the bend, he thought he'd have a laugh at the tortoise's expense. He lay down under a tree and pretended to nap – just to show that he could even stop to sleep and still beat the tortoise. But in the peaceful coolness, the hare really did fall fast asleep!

Slowly, slowly, the tortoise plodded on – past the sleeping hare – until the finish line was in sight. All at once the hare woke with a start, horrified. He bounded away, but the tortoise passed the finish line before he could catch up.

Slow and steady wins the race.

The Goose that Laid the Golden Eggs

Once upon a time, there lived a farmer who owned a prize goose. The goose laid an egg every day, which was always big and tasty. Once, when the farmer went to check the nest, he was surprised to find that the egg looked strange – it was yellow and shiny. When he picked it up, it was as heavy as lead.

The farmer's first thought was that an envious neighbour must have played a trick on him. But just before he threw the egg away, he thought better of it, and took it home instead. There, he examined it closely, and to his surprise he found that the egg was made of pure gold.

To the farmer's amazement, the next day the goose laid another golden egg... and the next day... and the next... He soon became wealthy from selling them. However, as he grew richer, he became greedier. One day he decided he had to have all the gold the goose must have inside her – so he killed her and opened her up, only to find nothing.

Greedy people who try to take too much will often run out of luck.

The Mischievous Dog

A man once had a dog that was a faithful, loyal companion to him. However, whenever visitors came to the man's house, the dog would bark and snap at them for no reason. The man of course found this a great nuisance – not to mention a danger – so he fastened a bell around the dog's neck. This way, as people approached his house, they would hear the dog coming and be warned to stay back.

The dog was very proud of the bell. He strutted about tinkling it with great satisfaction, showing it off as if it were a medal.

One day an old dog came up to him and said, "The fewer airs you give yourself the better, my friend. You don't think, do you, that your bell was given as a reward of merit? On the contrary, it is a badge of disgrace."

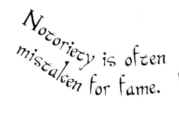

Notoriety is often mistaken for fame.

The Miser and his Gold

Once upon a time there lived a miserly man, whose greatest pleasure in life was to save his money and count it. Each day, he would lock the door to his house, draw the blinds, and fetch the chest of gold coins from under his bed. His eyes would glint and gleam as he placed the money into piles and counted up the total.

One day, as the man was counting the coins, an awful thought took hold of him. What if someone broke into his house one day while he was at market? They would surely look under the bed and find his treasure. But the old miser could not think of a better hiding place.

Then an idea came to him. "I know," he said to himself, "if there is not a better hiding place inside the house, perhaps outside the house would be safer."

That night, under cover of darkness, the man crept into his garden with a big spade. At the foot of the biggest tree he dug a deep hole, in which he placed his chest of gold. He covered the chest over with earth, then he crept back inside, rubbing his hands with glee.

From then on, every night, the man would steal into his garden and dig up the chest.

He would delight in counting the coins, then bury his treasure in the hole once more. The man thought he had been so clever — no one would come across it there.

However, little did the man know that on one particular night, a robber was hiding in the tree. He saw everything, and of course, as soon as the miser had returned inside his house, the robber came down from the tree, dug up the treasure and ran off with it.

The next night, when the man came outside to gloat over his treasure, he was horrified to find nothing but the empty hole. He wailed and wept and tore at his hair, and raised such an outcry that all his neighbours came running to see what had happened. Then the man owned up and told them about how he used to come and check on his gold.

"Did you ever spend any of it?" asked one neighbour.

"No," said the man, "I only counted it."

"Then come again and look at the hole," said a neighbour, "it will do you just as much good."

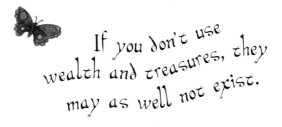

If you don't use wealth and treasures, they may as well not exist.

The Olive Tree and the Fig Tree

High on a hillside in a sunny country, an olive tree lived next to a fig tree. They had been neighbours for a long time, putting forth harvest after harvest of fruit. As the two stood surveying the landscape before them, they would chat. From time to time they would tease each other.

One day, the olive tree taunted the fig tree about how she lost her leaves every autumn.

"You lose your leaves each year when the weather turns colder, and you stay bare until the

spring. Whereas I, as you see,
stay green all year round."
For of course, olive trees
are evergreen.

It wasn't long after
that the frosts of winter came.
The weather was harsh and
there was a heavy fall of snow. The snow settled
on the tiny leaves of the olive tree like a thick
blanket — she was so bowed down with the
weight that her branches bent and broke. But
the snowflakes fell harmlessly through the bare
branches of the fig, which survived for many
more harvests.

People who boast about their
wealth or their fortune can meet
with unexpected disaster.

Mercury
and the
Woodman

Long, long ago in the early days of the world, the messenger god Mercury was walking through a forest when he heard someone groaning and moaning nearby. He hurried through the trees and found that the voice belonged to a woodman. The woodman had been felling a tree on the riverbank, when his axe had bounced off the trunk, flown out of his hands and fallen into the water. Now he stood by the water's edge lamenting his loss.

Mercury felt very sorry for the woodman. How

would he make a living without the tool of his trade? To the woodman's huge surprise, the god suddenly dived into the river. No sooner had Mercury plunged into the water than he reappeared — holding a golden axe.

"Is this what you lost?" he asked the woodman.

The woodman was of course tempted for a moment to reply that the amazing axe was his — but being an honest fellow he sighed, and did not.

Then Mercury dived a second time and brought up a silver axe, and asked if it was the woodman's.

"No, that is not mine either," said the woodman with another deep sigh.

Once more Mercury dived into the river, and this time he brought up the woodman's missing axe. The woodman was overjoyed at recovering his property, and thanked the god heartily. In turn, Mercury was so pleased with the woodman's honesty that he made him a present of the other two axes.

The woodman couldn't believe it. He hurried home and told the story to his friends – who were of course filled with envy. One of them was so jealous that he was determined to try his luck for himself.

The man went to the edge of the river and began to fell a tree, and presently let his axe drop into the water. Mercury appeared as before, and on learning that the axe had fallen in, he dived and again brought up a golden axe.

Without waiting to be asked if it was his or not the man cried, "That's mine, that's mine!" and stretched out his hand eagerly for the prize. But Mercury was so disgusted at his dishonesty that he not only took away the golden axe, he also refused to recover the one that had fallen into the river.

Honesty is the best policy.

The Shipwrecked Man and the Sea

Ashipwrecked man was struggling to survive in the cold, cruel sea. The gods were smiling on him though, for he managed to keep his head above the waves and was washed up on a beach. As soon as he felt his body rest upon the sand, he fell into a deep sleep.

When the man finally awoke, he was furious. He stood at the edge of the waves and raged at the sea – which was now as smooth as a millpond.

"How deceitful you are!" he raged. "You draw people in by showing your peaceful side, but when you have us in your power, you become cruel and punish us."

To his huge surprise, the sea then appeared before his eyes in the form of a woman, and replied, "Don't blame me, O sailor, it's the fault of the winds. By nature I am as calm and safe as the land itself, but the winds buffet me with their gusts and gales, and whip me into a monster."

Beware of people who are controlled by others.

The Boy
and the
Filberts

There was once a little boy who noticed a jar of nuts, or filberts, on a shelf. They looked so tasty that he couldn't resist reaching up and lifting them down. He took off the lid, thrust his hand inside the jar, and greedily grasped as many as he could hold.

But when he tried to pull his hand out again, he found he couldn't, for the neck of the jar was too small to allow such a large handful to get through. The little boy didn't want to let go of all his tasty treats, but unless he did, he couldn't get his hand out. The little boy burst into tears.

Just then a neighbour was passing by the window and saw what the trouble was. "There, there," she said. "Come, my boy, don't be so greedy. If you let go of some of the nuts and be content with just half of what you have, you'll be able to get your hand out easily enough."

Do not attempt too much at once.

The Blacksmith and his Dog

There was once a blacksmith who had a little dog, which used to sleep when its master was hard at work, sweating in his fiery furnace. However at mealtimes, the dog was always wide awake.

This used to drive the blacksmith quite mad, for he did not feel that the dog was earning its keep by doing anything useful. One day, the blacksmith snapped after throwing the dog a bone left over from his dinner, and he bellowed, "What use are you, you good-for-nothing animal? You don't keep watch for strangers or guard my smithy at all. When I am hammering away at my anvil, you just curl up and go to sleep. But no sooner do I stop for a mouthful of food than you wag your tail to be fed."

Those who will not work will not have enough food.

The Travellers and the Plane Tree

Two travellers were walking along a dusty road on a hot summer's day. They were relieved when they came across a broad plane tree, and turned off the road to shelter from the sun in the deep shade of its branches. They sank down and cooled off, and then got out some food to eat.

As the travellers rested, refreshed, they looked up into the tree and one of them remarked to his companion, "What a useless tree the plane is. It bears no fruit and is of no service to man at all."

Then the plane tree interrupted him with great indignation. "You ungrateful creature!" it cried. "You come and take shelter beneath me from the scorching sun, and then, in the very act of enjoying the cool shade I provide, you claim I am good for nothing!"

Many a service is met with ingratitude.

The Donkey
and the
Old Peasant

An old peasant was once travelling
with all his belongings strapped to donkey,
which he had been driving down the road by
hitting it with a stick.

The peasant decided to have a rest in a
nearby field, and was watching the donkey eating
a well-earned meal by grazing on the sweet
grass. All of a sudden he caught sight of armed
men stealthily approaching.

The terrified peasant leapt to his feet and
tried to jump onto the donkey's back, begging it

to run as fast as it could. "Hurry up, or else we will be captured by these thugs!"

But the donkey refused to budge. It just looked around lazily and said, "And if we are, do you think they'll make me carry heavier loads than I have to now?"

"Probably not," said the peasant.

"Oh well," said the donkey, "I don't mind if they do take me, for I shan't be any worse off." And it returned to nibbling the grass, leaving its master to his fate.

It's better to settle for the lesser of two evils.

The Sick Stag

A mighty stag was once the lord of the forest, held in awe and respected by all the other creatures that lived there.

However there came a time when the stag fell ill. He became so sick that he collapsed in a shady clearing, too weak to move from the spot. The birds flying overhead soon saw what had happened and talked about it in sadness. Soon other creatures heard too, and as the news of the stag's illness spread, many of the other forest beasts came to see how he was.

However as they came, they all nibbled a little of the grass that grew around the stag until there was not a blade within his reach.

After a few days the stag felt better, but by then he was too weak to go in search of food. And so it was that he died of hunger — due to the thoughtlessness of his friends.

Bad friends can do you more harm than good.

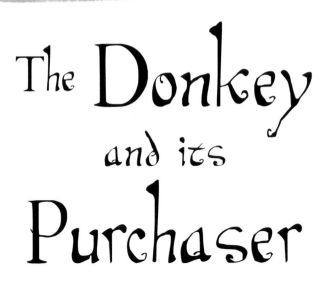

The Donkey
and its
Purchaser

There was once a trader whose business was booming. He already owned several donkeys to carry his wares to market, but he thought he needed another. So he went to town to buy one.

The trader came across a possible beast, but wasn't sure if the animal was right for the work. So he arranged with the owner to take the donkey home on trial to see what it was like.

Off went the trader with the donkey, and when he got home, he put the animal into the stable with the other donkeys. The newcomer looked around, and immediately chose a place next to the laziest, greediest beast in the stable.

When the trader saw this the next day, he at once led the donkey back to its owner. The owner was surprised to see him back so soon, and said, "You have tested the animal already? You haven't given it time to prove itself."

"That's enough for me," replied the trader. "I can see what sort of beast it is from the company it chose."

You are judged by the company you keep.

The Donkey Carrying the Statue

Once upon a time in a far-off city there was a procession to the temple of an important goddess. The city's best craftspeople had spent months carving a beautiful wooden statue of the goddess, which would be placed on display in the temple for all to worship.

The statue was carried at the head of the procession on the back of a donkey, surrounded by priests and priestesses and followed by hundreds of slaves chanting prayers and throwing rose petals. As the donkey passed along, crowds of people bowed low in front of the statue he carried. The foolish donkey thought the people were bowing their heads in a token of respect to him.

He bristled with pride, puffed out his chest, threw his head back and refused to move another step. But then the driver laid his whip on his rear quarters, shouting, "You idiot! How can you imagine that people would pay worship to a fool like you!"

It is not a wise move to take the credit due to other people.

The Thief
and the
Innkeeper

Once upon a time, a thief rented a room at an inn, and stayed there several days on the look-out for something to steal. However, no opportunity presented itself, until one day when the innkeeper appeared in a fine new coat.

The thief no sooner set eyes upon the coat than he longed to get his hands on it, so he took a seat in the garden by the innkeeper's side. They chatted amiably for some time, then the thief suddenly yawned and howled like a wolf.

The innkeeper was shocked and concerned,

and asked the thief what the matter was.

The thief replied, "I will tell you about myself, sir, but first I must beg you to take charge of my clothes for me, for I intend to leave them with you. Why I have these fits of yawning I cannot tell — maybe they are sent as a punishment for things I have done wrong. But the facts are that when I have yawned three times I become a raging wolf and fly at men's throats." As he finished speaking he yawned a second time and howled again as before.

The innkeeper, believing every word and terrified at the prospect of being confronted with a wolf, started to run indoors, but the thief caught him by the coat, crying, "Stay, sir, and take charge of my clothes, or I shall never see them again." As the thief spoke he opened his mouth and began to yawn for the third time.

The innkeeper, mad with fear, slipped out of his coat — which remained in the other's hands — and bolted inside. The thief then stole off with his spoil.

Don't always believe everything people say.

The Stag
and the Vine

A stag was once running for his life from some huntsmen. He plunged into a field and, feeling his limbs growing tired, looked desperately for somewhere to hide. He saw a thick vine growing nearby and raced behind it to take cover. Trying to calm the sound of his laboured breathing, he stood stone-still as the huntsmen raced past his hiding place – with no idea that the stag was there.

The stag waited for a while, then supposing all danger to be over, he began to munch on the leaves of the vine for refreshment. Little did he know that the huntsmen were not as far away as he thought. One keen-eyed hunter noticed the leaves of the vine moving, although there was no wind. He realized that an animal was hidden there and shot an arrow into the foliage.

The stag was pierced in the heart, and, as he died, he said, "I deserve my fate for feeding upon the leaves of my protector."

Ungratefulness sometimes brings its own punishment.

166

Challenge and Chance

The Wolf and the Lamb

Once upon a time, a wolf was on a hillside, lapping at the cool waters of a spring when, looking up, what should he see but a lamb having a drink a little lower down.

The wolf hadn't eaten for a day or two and the lamb was young and plump. 'There's my supper,' thought the starving wolf, 'and very tasty it looks too. If only I could find some way to get hold of it.'

The wolf stood quietly, watching the lamb splash in the water in the warmth of the sun. His back bristled with temptation and his stomach growled with hunger. He licked his lips and roared out angrily to the lamb, "Hey – you down there! Stop tramping about at the edge of the stream – you are muddying the water from which I am drinking!"

The lamb jumped back in shock at the sight of the wolf. "No, master, no!" he said, all of a tremble. "If the water is muddy up there, it can't be my fault, because it's flowing from you down to me here."

A drop of saliva fell from the wolf's drooling jaws. "Well then," he spat, "why did you call me insulting names this time last year? You know you did!"

"L-l-l-last y-y-y-year?" stammered the lamb, bewildered. "That couldn't have been me — I am only six months old, I wasn't alive last year."

"I don't care," snarled the wolf, "if it wasn't you, it must have been another of your family." And with that, he sprang down the hillside. In just three great bounds he had leapt upon the little lamb and in a few moments he was hungry no longer.

A tyrant will use any reason as a cause for his wickedness.

The Lion's Share

A lion once went hunting with a fox, a jackal and a wolf. The four hunters prowled and lurked and tracked until at last they came upon a huge stag in the depths of a forest. Working together, they took the stag totally unawares and claimed its life.

The hunters stood triumphant as the stag lay before them. But then they all began to wonder how they should share out their catch.

Just as an argument was about to break out, the lion threw back his head and gave a mighty roar. "Divide this stag up into quarters right NOW!" he bellowed, and the other leapt to it. When it was done, the lion snarled at the fox, the jackal and the wolf, who stood sulkily before him. "The first quarter is for me," he declared, "because I am King of the Beasts."

The fox, the jackal and the wolf looked at each other and shrugged – that was fair enough, they thought. But then the lion went on... "The second quarter is mine too, as I am the one sorting out the shares."

"But—"

"Hang on a minute—"

"Rubbish!" The fox, the jackal and the wolf began to grumble, but the lion took no notice and carried on.

"The third share should be mine because of the part I played in hunting the stag. As for the fourth quarter, well, I should like to see which of you will dare to lay a paw upon it." And the lion bared his teeth and flexed his sharp claws.

The three other hunters slunk away into the shadows with their tails between their legs.

Powerful people are more than happy to let you do some of their work, but they won't share the rewards.

The Fox
and the
Monkey

A fox and a monkey were once travelling together. They were chatting to pass the time, when they fell into an argument about which of them was the more noble creature.

"Of course, of the two of us, I am the grandest animal," said the fox. "I come from a line of brave and highly respected hunters."

174

"Surely I am the more noble of us," insisted the monkey, "for my family live high above yours, in the trees."

On and on they went, bickering away for quite some time, until they passed a cemetery. The cemetery was full of grand, beautifully carved monuments to the dead buried there.

The monkey looked around and fell quiet for a moment or two, thinking. Then he let out a big sigh.

"What on earth has made you sigh like that?" asked the fox.

The monkey pointed to the huge, expensive tombs all around and replied, "All the monuments that you see here were put up in honour of my fathers and my fathers' fathers, who in their day were very important."

The fox was speechless for a moment, but quickly recovered and said, "Oh! Please keep on with your lies – don't stop now. You're quite safe, no matter what ridiculous claims you make, because none of these poor souls can rise up and say that you're talking absolute rubbish!"

Boasters show off the most when no one can prove that they are lying.

The Four Oxen
and the
Lion

Once upon a time there were four oxen who lived in a field. A lion regularly used to prowl around, wondering how he could catch one of them to eat. Many a time the lion tried to attack the oxen, but whenever he came near, they all stood with their tails together.

In this way, from whichever direction the lion approached, he was met by the horns of one of the oxen – and very long, sharp horns they were too. Nevertheless, the determined lion returned again and again to try his luck.

One day, the oxen argued among themselves and fell out. Each of the stubborn animals stomped off to a different corner of the field to graze. Little did they know that the lion had chosen that very day to set out on another hunting attempt.

Imagine the lion's glee when he approached the field to see the oxen standing far apart, each one alone. His eyes gleamed as he weighed up which of the huge beasts to attack first – and then he sprang. No sooner had one fallen than he took down the second, the third, and then the last.

United we stand, divided we fall.

The Dog in the Manger

There was once a dog who was looking for a cosy place to take an afternoon nap. The horse was in the shade under the tree. The hen was curled up in the cart. The cat was basking in the sun on the barn roof.

The dog slunk into the barn and looked for a spot that was not yet taken. Suddenly his eyes came to rest on the ox's manger. It was filled with fresh, sweet-smelling hay. 'That's the place for me,' thought the dog, and he trotted over, jumped in and settled down to sleep.

A little later, the ox plodded into the barn. He was hot and tired from ploughing all day. After drinking at the water trough he went to his manger to eat, and found the dog fast asleep!

The ox's hot breath roused the dog from his dreams, and he jumped up, snarling. Each time the ox came near to try to take a mouthful of hay, the dog tried to bite him, even though he did not want to eat the hay himself. At last the ox was forced to give up and go away hungry.

People may not want others to have things, even if they can't use them themselves.

The One-eyed Doe

There once lived a doe who was chased by a hungry lion one day. She had been swift and nimble enough to escape the lion's jaws. But his claws had gouged one of her eyes and from then on, on that side, she was blind.

The doe was always nervous, for she could not see anyone approaching her on her blind side. So when she was grazing, she went to a high cliff near the sea. She positioned herself with her blind side near the cliff's edge, towards the ocean, so she could look out over the land with her good eye. This way, she could see if any hunters were approaching, and escape.

As time went by, more and more animals got to know that the doe was blind in one eye. Eventually some hunters came to hear of it too. They realized what the doe was up to and came up with a plan. The next day, the hunters hired a boat and rowed under the cliff where the doe was feeding. She never saw or heard them coming, and they shot her from the sea.

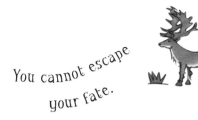

You cannot escape your fate.

The W*ind
and the Sun

Once a long time ago, the wind and the sun had an argument about which of them was the strongest.

"I am," said the sun, "for I can burn skin simply by staring at it."

"That may be," said the wind, "but I can toss boats on the waves just by breathing out."

Suddenly they saw below them a traveller on the road. Then the sun had an idea and said, "I see a way to settle this argument. Whichever of us can get that traveller to remove his cloak is the stronger."

The wind went first. He blew upon the traveller, harder and harder until trees bent against the force. But the traveller just, wrapped his cloak around him,

holding on to it tightly.

At last the wind gave up. Then the sun came beaming out and shone in all her glory upon the traveller. Immediately, the traveller relaxed his grip on his cloak. Still the sun blazed hotter until the traveller, wiping the sweat from his brow, was forced to take off his cloak entirely.

Kindness can be more effective than harshness.

The Lion, the Fox and the Beasts

The lion once fell ill – so ill that he was sure he was dying. He summoned all the animals to him so he could tell them his last wishes.

First, the goat came to the lion's cave. Trembling, he tottered in. He was gone a long time, so a sheep decided to go in to pay his respects. A calf waiting outside, also decided to enter the cave to hear the lion's last wishes.

After a while, the lion appeared from inside the gloom. Strangely, he was feeling stronger. He saw a fox waiting outside. "Why did you not come to see me?" he snarled.

"I beg your pardon," said the
fox, "but I noticed the tracks
of the animals that had
entered the cave.

And while I see many going in, I can't see any
coming out. Until all the animals that entered
the cave come out, I will stay here."

It is easier to get into an enemy's
clutches than to get out again.

The
Cat-maiden

Long, long ago, in the early days of the world, the great god Zeus ruled over the Earth. This did not stop the other gods and goddesses from arguing with him from time to time.

One day Venus, the goddess of beauty, was debating with Zeus if it was possible for a living thing to change its natural habits and instincts. Zeus said yes, it was – for instance, a camel could stop being bad-tempered if it so wished and be content and good-natured all the time. However, Venus said it was impossible – a camel could not stop being bad-tempered, just as a rabbit could not become fierce like a tiger, nor could a crocodile become vegetarian.

To test the question, Zeus turned a cat into a maiden, and gave her to a young man to take for his wife. The wedding was carried out with much rejoicing and celebration, and the young couple sat down to the wedding feast.

"See," said the mighty Zeus to the beautiful Venus, "how perfectly she behaves. Who could tell that yesterday she was but a cat? Surely her nature is changed?"

"Wait a minute," replied Venus, and with a flick of her fingers, she conjured up a mouse. No sooner did the bride see the mouse than she tried to pounce upon it.

"Ah, you see," said Venus. "You will have to agree that I am right after all!"

The true nature of a living thing will always show itself in the end.

The Horse, Hunter and Stag

Once upon a time, a horse and a stag were great friends. They often spent their days together, racing over the meadows. One day, a quarrel broke out over a small thing, and grew bigger and bigger until the friendship ended.

The horse dwelt on the argument, becoming more and more upset until he decided that only revenge would make him feel better. He asked a hunter for help.

The hunter listened thoughtfully as the horse explained how he wanted him to kill the stag.

"I will help you," the hunter said, "but to stand any chance of catching the stag, you must help me too. You must let me ride you."

Of course the horse agreed, and the hunter soon saddled and bridled him.

With the horse's speed, the hunter overcame the stag. Then the delighted horse said, "Many thanks! Now get off and remove those things from my mouth and back."

"Not so fast," said the hunter. "Now I've got you under bit and spur I will keep you that way."

If you allow people to use you to get what you want, they may also use you to get what they want.

The Lion and the Boar

O ne hot day, a lion and a boar came to a spring at the same time to drink. They argued as to who should drink first.

"I was here first," growled the boar.

"Not so," insisted the lion, "I arrived seconds before you."

"False!" said the boar.

"You should give way to me," countered

the lion, "as I am King of the Beasts."

The quarrel continued, until the lion and the boar suddenly charged at one another in a frenzy. They fought furiously until, pausing to take a breath, they saw some vultures seated on a rock above. The beady-eyed birds were obviously waiting for one of them to be killed so they could feed upon the dead carcass.

"If you're thinking what I'm thinking," said the lion, "we'd better make up."

"Yes," agreed the boar, "I'd rather forget our quarrel and live, than fight to the death and be food for vultures."

Those who argue and fight may be watched by others, who will take advantage of the loser to do better for themselves.

The Donkey
and its
Shadow

Long ago, there was a man who wanted to leave his home in the city and move to another, some distance away.

In order to take all his possessions with him, he hired a donkey, for he had too much to carry. He struck a deal with the donkey's owner, who would load the animal, and come on the journey to drive the donkey and feed and water it.

All went well to begin with – the owner arrived with the donkey, and loaded it up. They set off down the road, making good progress

until the sun
blazed overhead
and they were forced to
stop and rest.

The traveller wanted to lie
down in the donkey's shadow,
but the owner wouldn't let him —
he said he had hired the donkey, not its shadow.
The traveller argued that his bargain gave him
control of the donkey... and so the argument
went on. The quarrel grew heated, until they
came to blows. Of course, while the men were
fighting, the donkey took to its heels and was
soon out of sight.

If you quarrel about something
that is unimportant, you may well lose
what is important.

The Goat and the Vine

A goat wandered into a vineyard one day, where the vines grew strong and thick, and were dripping with the juiciest grapes. She couldn't believe her luck at having stumbled upon such a delicious treat, and at once trotted over to the nearest stems and began to graze on the tender green shoots.

All of a sudden, the goat heard a voice moaning. She looked all around but no one was near. Then she realized with a start that it was the vine itself.

"Whatever have I done to you for you to hurt me like this?" it sobbed. "Isn't there enough grass for you to feed on?"

Before the goat could reply, the vine said, "But even if you eat every leaf and leave me bare, I will still produce wine for the cook to add to the pot when you are being cooked as a stew."

If you cross somebody, you can be certain they will want to get their own back.

199

The Lioness
and the
Vixen

A lioness and a vixen were once talking about their young, as mothers often do, and praising everything about them.

"My children are the picture of health," said the vixen, "I have had many compliments on how big and strong they are growing."

"Well, my child has a particularly splendid coat," said the lioness, "and his mane is clearly going to be

200

quite a sight to see once he reaches adulthood."

"Everyone tells me how my children are the image of their parents," said the vixen proudly.

"And I am often told that my son is clearly going to be as strong and courageous as his father," insisted the lioness.

"When I see my litter of cubs playing together, it's an absolute joy to behold," said the vixen, then she added, rather maliciously, "but I notice you never have more than one."

"That's true," said the lioness with a steely glint in her eye, "but that one grows up to be the King of the Beasts."

Quality, not quantity.

The Hound and the Hare

There was once a young
hound who sniffed out a
hare and chased her at full pelt until
he had caught up with her.

The hare was terrified, waiting
for death and wondering why
the hound did not finish her
off. One moment he would lunge at
her and snap with his teeth as though he
were about to kill her – even grabbing her coat
in his jaws. Then the next, he would let her go

and leap about playfully, as if having fun with another dog.

The tormented hare grew more desperate until at last she gasped, "I wish you would show your true colours. If you are my friend, why do you bite me? If you are my enemy, why do you play with me?"

Anyone who plays double is not a true friend.

203

The Wild Boar and the Fox

One fine day, a fox was wandering through a forest, minding his own business, when he came across a wild boar. The boar was hard at work rubbing his white tusks against the bark of a tree to make them fine and sharp.

The fox looked all around. Then he sniffed the air. But he could neither see nor smell any hunters that the boar might need to fight off — nor indeed any other dangers.

"My friend, why are you doing that?" asked the fox. "I cannot think of a reason why you are so hard at work preparing your tusks for battle."

"True, comrade," replied the boar. "But the instant my life is in danger I shall need my tusks. There'll be no time to sharpen them then."

Be prepared.

The Three Tradesmen

Once upon a time, the people of a certain city decided that they should build a high, strong wall all around it to keep their enemies out. They held a meeting to which all were invited, so that everyone could put forward their ideas and agree a plan of action.

At the start of the meeting, a carpenter stood up and recommended that the wall should be built of wood. "There are many dense forests round about," he argued, "so wood is in plentiful supply — and it's an easy material to work with."

"I beg to differ, my friend," contended a stonemason. "It is not a good idea to build a city wall from wood as it could be easily burnt down. I say that we would be better off using stone."

"No, I have to disagree with you both," cried a leather-worker, getting to his feet. "The best material would be hides — in my opinion there's nothing like leather."

People will always look after their own interests — every man for himself.

The Dog
and the
Wolf

It was a hot day on the farm, and the dog was on guard at the gate. He was having trouble staying awake. The flies were buzzing drowsily, and from the fields came the sound of cows mooing and sheep bleating contentedly. The dog's attention faded. First one eye drooped, then the other.

Then, out of nowhere, a wolf pounced! Suddenly, the dog was fighting for his life.

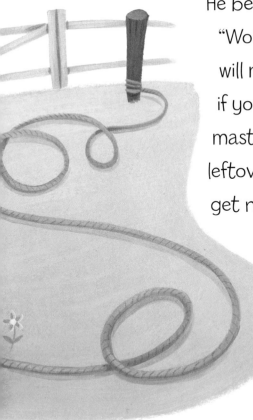

He begged for mercy, saying, "Wolf, you see how thin I am? I will make a wretched meal. But if you wait a few days, my master is giving a feast. The leftovers will be mine and I shall get nice and fat. This will be a better time to eat me." So the wolf just snarled and sloped away.

As the dog had said, the feast took

place and he ate his fill of tasty leftovers. The next day, the wolf arrived, only to find the dog out of reach on the stable roof.

"My friend," the dog said, "if you catch me down there again, don't wait for any feast."

Once bitten, twice shy.

The Wolf, the Fox and the Ape

There was once a time when a wolf and a fox were firm friends. They went hunting together and shared whatever food they caught between them. However one day, an argument arose between them.

The wolf caught a deer on a mountainside and left it lying on the rocks while he went to drink at a stream. When he returned from quenching his thirst, the body of the deer had vanished – and the fox was lurking nearby. In his fury, the wolf accused the fox of stealing the deer from him – which the fox strongly denied. Each animal accused and insulted the other, and neither would back down. So they agreed to take their argument to someone else to judge.

The wolf and the fox presented their grievances to an ape, who listened carefully to each of them, and then announced, "I do not think that you, dear wolf, ever lost the body of a deer, as you say you did. But all the same I believe that you, dear fox, are guilty of the theft, in spite of all your denials."

The dishonest get no credit, even if they act honestly.

Schemes and Dreams

The Fox
and the
Crow

Acrow once spied a piece of cheese on the ground. She swooped down and picked it up in her beak. Then she flew to a nearby tree, where she settled on a branch.

A fox was lurking in some bushes nearby and saw what she had done. He licked his lips at the thought of the delicious cheese.

The fox strolled up to the foot of the tree and cried, " Mistress Crow,

how well you look today, how glossy your feathers, how bright your eyes. I'm sure your voice must be just as beautiful. Sing for me, please, so I can tell everyone that you are the Queen of Birds."

The crow was thrilled by these words. She lifted her head and began to caw – and the cheese fell to the ground.

The fox pounced on it at once, snapping it up in his jaws. "That was all I wanted," he said. "In exchange for your cheese I will give you a piece of advice — when people pay you compliments, they may not be telling the truth."

Do not trust flatterers.

The Bat, the Birds and the Beasts

There was once a time when the birds and the beasts always argued. After a while, things had got so bad between them that the two sides decided to wage war on each other. When the armies were ready, the bat hesitated about which to join. The birds that passed his perch said, "Come with us."

But the bat said, "I am a beast."

Later on, some beasts who were passing said, "Come with us."

But the bat said, "I am a bird."

At the last moment peace was made between the two sides, and no battle took place. The bat heard the sound of celebrations and went to look — it was the birds, rejoicing.

"Can I join the party?" he asked, but the birds flew at him angrily and he had to fly away.

As he flew, he came across the beasts, who were also having a party. The bat swooped down and said, "May I join in?" But the beasts charged at him furiously, and he had to flee again.

"I see," said the bat, "I did not say I was one thing or the other, so now I don't fit anywhere."

He that is neither one thing or the other has no friends.

The Vain Jackdaw

Long ago, the great god Jupiter ruled over the Earth. One day, he was looking down over all creation when he saw that the birds were arguing and squabbling amongst themselves.

'This will not do,' thought Jupiter. 'There must be a way that they can keep order amongst themselves.'

Jupiter thought hard, and finally came up with an idea. He announced that he intended to appoint a king of the birds, to rule over them and keep control. The god named a day

on which all the birds were to appear before his throne, when he would select the most beautiful to be their ruler.

The birds were hugely excited – all of them wished to be chosen. Wanting to look their best, they hurried off to the banks of a stream, where they busied themselves in bathing and preening. The jackdaw was also there, but he realized that, with his ugly plumage, he would have little chance. So he waited until the others

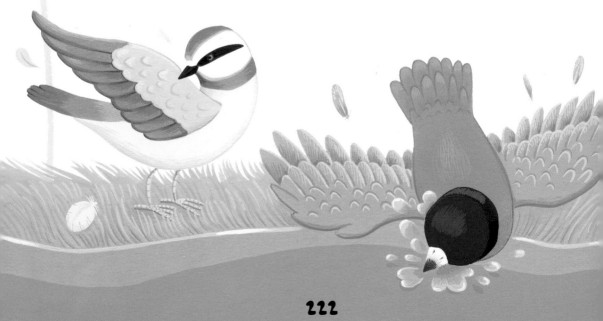

had gone, and then picked up the brightest of the feathers they had dropped, and stuck them all over his own body. When he had finished, he looked at his reflection in the water – he was very pleased with his handiwork.

When the day came, the birds assembled before Jupiter. One bird caught the eye of the great god because of its colourful plumage – the jackdaw. But just as Jupiter was about to

make him king, the other birds turned on the jackdaw stripped him of his feathers, and exposed him for the unremarkable bird that he really was.

Dressing up does not make you a better, more worthy person.

The Fox, the Rooster and the Dog

One moonlit night, a fox was prowling about a farmyard. He could sniff delicious smells coming from the hen-coop. He made his way silently towards it and saw a rooster perched nearby. The fox quickly thought of a plan and cried, "Good news, good news!"

"Why, what is it?" asked the rooster.

"King Lion has declared that all the animals should live in peace," declared the fox. "From now on, no beast may hurt another, but we must all live together in brotherly friendship."

"Why, that is good news," said the rooster, "and I see someone coming with whom we can share it." And so saying he craned his neck forward and pretended to stare closely at something.

"What is it you see?" said the fox.

"My master's dog is coming towards us," the rooster said. The fox began to turn away.

"Will you not stop and congratulate the dog on the reign of peace?" questioned the rooster.

"I would gladly do so," said the fox, "but I fear he may not have heard of King Lion's decree."

Cunning often outwits itself.

The Tortoise
and the
Birds

Once upon a time, there was a tortoise who wanted to find somewhere new to live. He wasn't exactly sure where – all he knew was that he was fed up where he was and wanted a change. He thought that if the eagle picked him up, she would be able to carry him high up in the sky from where he could look down and see all the land below. Then he would be able to decide where he wanted to live.

So he asked the eagle if she would help him, and promised her a rich reward for her trouble.

The eagle agreed, and seizing the tortoise by the shell with her talons, she soared aloft.

As the eagle flew over the landscape, they met a crow, who said to the eagle, "Tortoise is good for eating."

"Ah yes," said the eagle in reply. "But the shell is much too tough."

"Those rocks would crack the shell," was the crow's answer, nodding down below.

And the eagle, taking the hint, let the tortoise fall down onto the sharp rocks. Then the two birds made a meal of him.

Never soar aloft on
an enemy's wings.

229

The Impostor

There was once a man who fell ill and became so sick that he thought he might die. He prayed to the gods to help him, and promised that, if they would make him better, he would sacrifice one hundred oxen to them.

High up on Mount Olympus, the gods were curious to see how the man would keep this extravagant promise. So they made him recover in double-quick time.

Of course the man didn't have one ox, let alone one hundred. So he came up with a

230

cunning plan. He made one hundred little oxen out of wax and offered them up to the gods.

The gods were furious. They were determined to get even with the man, so one night they sent him a dream in which he was told to go to the seashore and fetch one hundred gold coins, which he would find there.

The next day, the man hurried to the shore. However once there, a band of robbers captured him and carried him off to sell as a slave. The price he fetched was one hundred gold coins.

Do not promise more than you can deliver.

The Fox Without a Tail

Once upon a time, a wily fox caught his tail in a trap. He struggled and struggled to get free, and as he twisted and turned he broke loose — but his tail was left behind.

The fox was mightily relieved. However, his relief soon turned to embarrassment about no longer having a tail. He felt so ashamed, he did not want to show himself in public. But he was determined to put a bold face upon his misfortune, and summoned all the foxes to a meeting.

When everyone had assembled, the fox showed them that he was tailless. Then he proposed that all foxes should do away with their tails. He pointed out how inconvenient a tail was when they were pursued by dogs. The fox reminded them that it was in the way when they wanted to sit down. He said that there was no point in carrying around something so useless.

"That is all very well," said one of the older foxes, "but I do not think you would have asked us to do away with our beautiful brushes if you had not lost yours."

Do not trust interested advice.

The Wolf in Sheep's Clothing

There was once a wolf who kept trying to
steal sheep from a flock. However, the
shepherd and sheepdogs were very watchful
and always chased him away. But the wolf
did not give up. He hung around,
waiting for a chance.

His chance came
one day when he found a
sheepskin that had been cast
aside. He put it over his coat and
tied it around him, so he was

quite disguised. Then he strolled among the sheep – none of them noticed anything strange. In fact, the lamb of the sheep whose skin the wolf was wearing began to follow the wolf.

Leading the lamb away from the flock, the wolf made a meal of her. And for some time afterwards, he succeeded in deceiving the sheep, the shepherd and the sheepdogs, and enjoying hearty meals.

Appearances can be deceptive.

The Cat
and the Mice

Once there was a house that was overrun with mice. A cat heard of this, and said to herself, "That's the place for me," and off she went to live there. Every day, the cat caught the mice one by one and ate them.

After a week, the mice had lost so many of their friends they could stand it no longer. They decided to stay in their holes and not come out until the cat gave up and went away.

'Hmm,' thought the cat. 'The only thing to do is to trick them out.' So she came up with a plan.

The cat climbed up the wall then grasped a peg with her hind legs, lowering her body until she was hanging upside down. She pretended to be dead. The cat thought the mice would be fooled and come out.

By and by, a mouse peeped out and saw her hanging there. But it wasn't taken in.

"Aha!" it cried. "You're very clever, but you won't catch us anywhere near you."

Don't be deceived by the innocent ways of those whom you have once found to be dangerous.

The Milkmaid and her Pail

Once upon a time, a milkmaid was walking to market, carrying her milk in a pail on her head. She began to plan what she would do with the money she would get for the milk.

"I think I'll buy some chickens from Farmer Brown," she said, "and they will lay eggs each morning, which I can sell to the parson's wife. With the money that I get from the eggs, I'll buy myself a new dress and a new hat, and when I go to market, all the young men will come up and speak to me! Polly Shaw will be jealous... but I don't care. I shall just look at her and toss my head like this."

As she spoke she tossed her head back, the pail fell off, and all the milk was spilled.

Do not count your chickens before they are hatched.

The Donkey, the Fox and the Lion

There was once a donkey and a fox who decided that they could find more food if they went into partnership.

So they set out to look for something to eat, but they hadn't gone far before they saw a lion coming their way. They were both dreadfully frightened. But while the donkey looked around for a place to hide, the fox thought he saw a way of saving his own skin.

He dashed up to the lion and whispered in his ear, "If you promise to let me go free, I shall make sure that you get the donkey without going to any trouble." The lion agreed, so the fox scampered back to his companion.

The fox pretended that he had found a hiding place and led the donkey towards the forest. On the way, the fox took the donkey over a pit that a hunter had dug as a trap for wild animals. The donkey fell down into the pit.

When the lion saw that the donkey was trapped, he immediately pounced on the fox and gobbled him up. Then he had all the time in the world to feast upon the donkey.

If you betray a friend, you should expect to be betrayed yourself.

Belling
the Cat

Long ago, a group of mice were terrorized by a cat. Every day, the cat made their life a misery by hiding roundabout, spying on their holes and waiting for them to come out.

The mice held a meeting to discuss how they could outwit the cat. Some said this, and some said that, but at last a young mouse got up and said he had a proposal to put forward.

242

"You will all agree," he said, "that our danger lies in the sly way in which the enemy lurks about, waiting for us. If we could receive some signal of her approach, we could easily escape. I therefore propose that we get a small bell and attach it round the neck of the cat. Then we will always know when she is about."

This proposal met with a lot of clapping, until an old mouse got up and said, "But who is going to volunteer to tie the bell on the cat?"

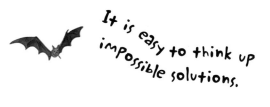

It is easy to think up impossible solutions.

243

The Sheep, the Wolf and the Stag

There was once a stag who wanted to plant a field of wheat. He knew that the sheep had some wheat, so he asked her if she would lend him a measure until the following year. The stag told the sheep not to worry if he was unable to pay back the wheat at the appointed time, as his friend the wolf would pay.

The sheep, however, was afraid that the stag and the wolf meant to cheat her. She told the stag no, saying, "The wolf is in the habit of seizing what he wants and running off without paying, and you, too, can run much faster than I. So when the debt is due, how shall I be able to catch either of you?"

Your faults are not excused by the faults of someone else.

The Stag
and the
Lion

A **stag was once being chased** by hounds. As he grew tired, he looked around desperately for a hiding place. At last, the stag saw a cave where he hoped he would be safe from his pursuers. He dashed inside, panting furiously.

Unfortunately, a lion lived in the cave and the stag was completely at his mercy.

Realizing his fate

the stag cried, "I am saved from the power of the dogs only to fall into the clutches of a lion."

Out of the frying pan into the fire.

247

The Fox and the Cat

There was once a fox and a cat who were discussing what was the best way to escape from enemies. The fox was boasting about how he always outwitted his enemies.

"I have a whole bag of tricks," the fox said, "which contains a hundred different ways of escaping."

"Well, I have only one method of escape," said the cat, "but I can generally manage with that."

At that very moment the fox and the cat heard the cry of hounds. They looked at each other in horror, then the cat scampered up a tree and hid herself in the thick, leafy boughs.

"This is my plan of escape," she said to the fox. "What are you going to do?"

The fox thought first of one way, then of another... And while he was wondering which would be best to choose, the hounds got nearer and nearer... The fox was so caught up in confusion that he did nothing at all. The hounds caught him and he was killed by the huntsmen.

Better one safe way than a hundred that you cannot be sure of.

The Eagle, the Cat and the Wild Sow

In the middle of a forest there was an enormous old tree. At the very top, an eagle built her nest. In a hollow halfway down the trunk, a cat settled in with her family. And in the tangle of roots at the bottom lived a sow and her little piglets.

All the creatures might have got on very well as neighbours if it hadn't been for the cunning of the cat. Climbing up to the eagle's nest she said to the eagle, "You and I are in the greatest possible danger. That dreadful creature the sow,

who is always grubbing away at the foot of the tree, means to uproot it, so that she may gobble up both your family and mine." At this, the eagle was driven almost out of her mind with terror.

Then the cat climbed down the tree, and said to the sow, "I must warn you against that dreadful bird, the eagle. She is just waiting for her chance to swoop down and carry off one of your little piglets to feed her brood with." The cat succeeded in scaring the sow just as much as the eagle.

Then she returned to her hole in the trunk, from which, pretending to be afraid, she never came out by day. Only by night did she creep out unseen to find food for her kittens.

The eagle, meanwhile, was afraid to stir from her nest, and the sow dared not leave her home among the roots. In time, both they and their

families perished of hunger, and the cat and her family had the tree all to themselves.

Those who stir up suspicion and hatred are not to be trusted.

The Grasshopper
and the Owl

There was once an owl who lived in a hollow tree. She fed by night and slept by day, as all owls do. But whenever she was trying to sleep, her slumbers were greatly disturbed by the chirping of a grasshopper, who had made his home on a log beneath the tree.

The owl tossed and turned and tried everything she could think of to block out the grasshopper's singing and get to sleep. But nothing was any good. The owl begged the grasshopper repeatedly to have some

254

consideration and stop chirping, but the grasshopper, if anything, only sang louder.

At last the owl could stand it no longer, and was determined to rid herself of the pest by means of a trick. She said to the grasshopper, in the most pleasant way she could, "As I cannot sleep for your song, which is as sweet as harp music, I have a mind to taste some nectar. Won't you come in and join me?"

The grasshopper was flattered by the praise of his song, and his mouth watered at the mention of the delicious drink, so he said he would be

delighted. No sooner had he got inside the hollow where the owl was waiting than she pounced upon him and ate him up.

Do not let flattery throw you off your guard against an enemy.

The Father and his Daughters

Once upon a time, there lived a man who had two daughters. He loved them very much and wanted to see them live happy lives. One grew up to marry a gardener, while the other married a potter.

After a time, the man thought he would go and visit his daughters. First, he went to the gardener's wife. He asked her how things were going with herself and her husband. She replied that on the whole they were very well. "But," she continued, "I wish we could have some heavy rain.

The garden wants it badly. All our fruit and vegetables are about to wither and die."

Then the man went to the potter's wife. She said that she and her husband had nothing to complain of. "But," she went on, "I wish we could have some dry weather, to dry the pottery."

Her father looked at her, bemused. "You want dry weather," he said, "and your sister wants rain. I was going to ask in my prayers that your wishes be granted, but now it strikes me I had better not refer to the subject."

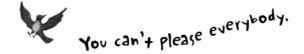

You can't please everybody.

The Bat, the Bramble and the Seagull

A bat, a bramble, and a seagull once fancied themselves as businessmen and dreamed of being rich. They went into partnership and decided to go on a trading voyage together. The bat borrowed some money for the trip, the bramble brought a stock of clothes, and the seagull gathered an amount of lead, and so they set out.

They loaded a ship with their cargo and sailed away. By and by they sailed into a great storm. The wind buffeted the boat and the waves battered it until great holes appeared. The boat, with all the cargo, sank to the bottom of the sea. Luckily, the three travellers managed to stay afloat and were washed onto the shore.

Ever since then, the seagull flies to and fro over the sea, and every now and then dives below the surface, looking for the lead he's lost. The bat is so afraid of meeting the money-lenders he borrowed from that he hides away by day and only comes out at night. And the bramble catches hold of the clothes of everyone who passes by, hoping some day to recognize and recover its lost garments.

People care more about recovering what they have lost than acquiring what they lack.

The **Wily Lion**

There was once a lion who came across a fat
bull feeding in a meadow. The lion watched
and waited, his mouth watering as he thought of
the feast he could make. But he dared not
attack for he was afraid of the bull's sharp horns.

However, the lion grew more and more hungry.
He knew that if he tried to pounce, he wouldn't
be successful, so he resorted to cunning instead.
He went up to the bull and said, "I cannot help
but admire your magnificent figure. What a
fine head. What powerful shoulders. But, my

friend, what in the world makes you wear those ugly horns? You must find them awkward. Believe me, you would do much better without them."

The bull was foolish enough to be swayed by this flattery, and the next day he had his horns cut off. Of course then he had lost his means of defence — and fell easy prey to the lion.

Beware of flatterers — they often want something.

Mad Mistakes

The Dog
and his
Reflection

Once upon a time there was a dog who had a piece of meat. He was carrying it home in his mouth to eat in peace. On his way, he came across a running brook and decided to trot along beside it.

As the dog walked along he looked down at the water, then stopped in surprise. There was another dog with a piece of meat in the water! The dog had no idea it was his own reflection. His only thought was that he had to have the other piece of meat too. So he made a snap at the dog in the water, but as he opened his mouth he dropped the meat. It plopped into the brook and was swirled away downriver.

It is very foolish to be greedy.

The Man
and the
Serpent

There was once a farmer who had a little boy, who was the joy of his life. The child was playing in the fields one day when by accident he trod on a serpent's tail. The angry creature turned and bit the boy.

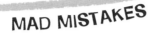

Within hours, he became very ill, and the next day he died.

The farmer was filled with anger and grief. He grabbed his axe and went out into the fields, determined to find the serpent no matter how long it took. After much searching, he found its lair and waited outside. As soon as the serpent came out, the farmer swung at it with his axe. The serpent was too quick for the farmer to kill it, but he managed to cut off a part of its tail.

Of course the serpent was now furious too. To get its own back, it began biting the farmer's cattle, which all died just as the little boy had. When the farmer began losing his herd, he realized his anger had got the better of him. As much as he didn't want to, he realized that he would have to make up with the serpent.

The farmer took some food and honey to the

mouth of the serpent's lair and said, "Let's forgive and forget. Perhaps you were right to punish my son and take vengeance on my cattle, but I thought I was right in trying to revenge my child. Now that we are both satisfied, why can't we be friends?"

But the serpent flicked out its tongue and turned to slither away. "No, no," it said, "take your gifts away. You will never forget the death of your son, nor I the loss of my tail."

Injuries may be forgiven, but not forgotten.

The
Grasshopper
and the Ants

It was proving to be a long, hard winter and all the animals were suffering from the cold, the damp and the lack of food.

There was one particularly long spell of rain that seemed to go on for days on end. Then at last the sun came out one day and brightened up the winter bleakness. As the hot rays warmed the ground, the wet earth steamed and sent up clouds of mist. Some ants came out from their mound, bringing their store of corn, grain by grain. It had got rather damp so they decided to lay it out in the sun to dry.

As the ants were hard at work fetching and carrying, along came a grasshopper who begged them to spare him a few grains, "For," he said, "I'm simply starving."

The ants stopped work for a moment, though this was against their instincts. "May we ask," they said, "what you were doing with yourself all last summer? Why didn't you collect a store of food for the winter?"

"The fact is," replied the grasshopper, "I was so busy singing that I didn't have the time."

"If you spent the summer singing," replied the ants, "you can't do better than spend the

MAD MISTAKES

winter dancing." And they chuckled and went on with their work.

It is best to be prepared in case hard times arrive.

The Donkey
and the
Mule

Once upon a time, there lived a man who owned a donkey and a mule. One day, he loaded them up and set off on a journey.

Where the road was level, the donkey plodded on without a problem. But eventually they came to where the road was rough and steep. The donkey found it hard going. It struggled on until it was gasping for breath.

On the verge of collapse, the donkey begged the mule to carry part of its load, but the unkind mule refused. At last, the exhausted donkey stumbled and fell down a cliff to its death.

The owner was in despair at the loss of his animal, as he now had the problem of how to carry on with his journey. In the end, he did the only thing possible – he climbed down and retrieved the donkey's load, and piled it on top of the mule's.

The mule could only just manage the extra weight, and, as it staggered painfully along, it said, "I have only got what I deserve – if I had helped the donkey, I would not be carrying this extra load into the bargain."

Prevention is better than cure.

The Donkey
and the
Lapdog

O ne day, a farmer went to his stables to check on his animals — among them his favourite donkey.

The farmer's lapdog went with him, and it danced about and licked its master's hand, as happy as could be. The farmer felt in his pocket, gave the lapdog a small snack, and sat down while he gave orders to his sons. The lapdog jumped onto its master's lap and lay there blinking while the farmer stroked its ears.

Upon seeing this, the donkey was filled with

jealousy, and wanted to be stroked and petted by the farmer too. So with a great pull, it broke loose from its halter and began prancing about just like the lapdog. At this sight, the farmer began laughing so hard that his sides ached.

The donkey thought that if the farmer was enjoying these antics so much, it must be doing a good job. So it went up to him, put its feet on his shoulders and tried to climb onto its master's lap.

When the farmer's sons saw the donkey squashing their father they rushed over with sticks and pitchforks. The donkey soon realized that fooling around so much that it hurt someone was not funny at all.

Clumsy jesting is no joke.

The Lion in Love

There was once a mighty lion who happened to fall in love with a beautiful maiden.

So the King of the Beasts went to the girl's parents to ask for her hand in marriage.

The parents were stunned – this was not what they had expected. They did not wish to give their daughter to the lion, yet they did not wish to enrage the King

279

of the Beasts either.

At last the father said, "We feel honoured by Your Majesty's proposal, but our daughter is only a girl, and we fear that you might injure her by accident. May we suggest that you have your claws removed and your teeth pulled out. Then we will consider your proposal again."

The lion was downhearted at first. But he was so much in love that he did indeed have his claws trimmed and his big teeth taken out.

Then the lion went again to see the parents of his beloved, with high hopes that this time they would agree to let her marry him. But of course, this time they just laughed in his face, for now they had no reason to be afraid of him.

Love can tame the wildest.

The
Boy who
Cried Wolf

There was once a shepherd boy who tended his sheep at the foot of a mountain near a dark forest. He was out on the slopes all day by himself, and he often got lonely and bored.

One day, the shepherd boy thought up a plan whereby he could get a little company and some excitement. He left his flock unattended and rushed down the slopes towards his village. He pretended to be in a terrible panic and shouted, "Wolf! Wolf!" at the top of his voice.

The villagers came running to check that he was unharmed. When they realized there was no wolf, they returned grumbling, telling the boy not to shout at false alarms.

A few days later the naughty boy tried the same trick again. He ran down the mountainside screaming, "Wolf! Wolf!" And again the villagers came rushing to help him. This time they were angry to find there was no wolf, just like the first time.

Just a few days later, the shepherd boy was watching his flocks as usual when a wolf really did come out of the forest and begin prowling around the sheep. Of course the boy set off down the mountainside crying, "Wolf! Wolf!"

even louder and in more of a panic than before.

But this time the villagers, who had already been fooled twice, thought the boy was again deceiving them. Nobody stirred to come to his aid. And so the wolf made a good meal of the boy's flock.

A liar will not be believed, even when he speaks the truth.

The Man and the Wood

Once upon a time, a man came striding boldly into a wood with an axe head in his hand. The trees were all nervous at first, for men with axes were one of their worst fears. However, they soon decided that the man was harmless enough. He did nothing at all except stand in a clearing, look around at all the trees, and beg them to give him one small branch, which he said he wanted for a particular job.

The trees overcame their fears and, being good-natured, gave him a stout, short branch.

However, what did the man do but put the branch straight into his axe head to use it as a dangerous tool. He began cutting down tree after tree. Then the trees saw how foolish they had been in giving their enemy the means to destroy them.

Beware what you give to potential enemies.

The Donkey
in the
Lion's Skin

Once upon a time, some hunters
caught and killed a lion. They skinned
the mighty beast and left its hide out in the sun
to dry while they set off on another hunt.
While the hunters were away, a
donkey came wandering by. He was
delighted to find the lion's skin
and thought he would try it
on. He put it over his head and
shoulders and was sure that
he looked good.

The donkey decided that finders were keepers, and he set off for home, draped in the hide. As he approached the village, everyone thought that a lion was approaching. People and animals alike fled as the donkey plodded closer.

The donkey realized what was happening, and was delighted. He lifted up his head with pride and brayed aloud. But that was a huge mistake — everyone realized who he was. Before he knew it, the villagers were pelting him with rotten vegetables for the trouble he had caused.

Fine clothes may disguise, but silly words will reveal a fool.

The Fox
and the
Goat

Once upon a time, an unfortunate fox fell into an unused well. The sides were steep and the well was too deep for him to climb out of. The fox was left helpless at the bottom, although thankful that the water had dried up.

At first the fox shouted for help, but nobody came, and after a while his voice grew tired. So he sat patiently, waiting for help to arrive, talking to himself from time to time.

Eventually a goat came past the well and heard the voice coming up from its depths.

Curious, he peered over and saw the fox, and asked what he was doing down there. "Oh, have you not heard?" replied the fox. "There is going to be a great drought, so I jumped down here to find some water in this old well. Why don't you come down as well?"

The goat considered the fox's words and decided that they made good sense, so he jumped down into the well too. However, the fox immediately jumped on the goat's back and, by putting his paws on her horns, managed to jump up to the top of the well.

"Goodbye, friend," called the fox, trotting off to freedom and leaving the goat trapped below.

Never trust the advice of a person in difficulties.

The Old Man
and
Death

There was once a man who had grown so old that he was bent double through old age and hard work. He lived on his own and had to do everything himself — from cooking his meals to repairing his little house.

One day he was out in the forest, gathering sticks for firewood, when his body began aching unbearably. The old man felt so tired and hopeless that he threw down the bundle of sticks and cried out, "I cannot bear this life any longer. I wish death would come and take me."

Just after he spoke, death — in the form of a skeleton — appeared and said to him, "What would you like of me, mortal? I heard you call me."

The man's face turned white and he gulped with fear. "Please, sir," he replied, "would you kindly help me to lift this bundle of sticks onto my shoulder?"

We would often be sorry if our wishes were granted.

The Buffoon
and the
Countryman

Once upon a time there was a country fair at which people were entertained with rides, competitions, stalls and fun shows.

One of the shows was performed by a buffoon, who made the crowds laugh by imitating various animals. He mooed like a cow, brayed like a donkey, roared like a lion and squawked like a parrot. He finished off by squealing so much like a pig that the spectators thought he had a pig hidden about him. But a countryman who stood by said, "Call that a pig's squeal? It's nothing like it. Give me until tomorrow and I will show you what it's like."

Sure enough, the next day the countryman appeared on stage. He put his head down and began squealing like a pig – but the noise was so dreadful that the crowd hissed and booed at him to make him stop.

The countryman grew red-faced. "You fools!" he cried. "See what you were hissing," and held up a little pig that he had been pinching to make it squeal.

People often applaud an imitation and hiss the real thing.

The Donkey, the Rooster and the Lion

Once upon a time, a donkey and a rooster were in a farmyard together when a lion came prowling by. He had not eaten for days and was ravenous, so had set his sights upon the donkey first, as a more satisfying meal. The lion was just about to pounce when the rooster crowed at the top of its voice, "Cockadoodledoo!"

It is said that the one thing lions are afraid of is a rooster's crow, and this lion certainly fled as fast as he could. The donkey decided that the

lion must be very
cowardly indeed, and
galloped after him to
attack him himself.
However the lion heard the
donkey galloping behind him – and of
course he wasn't frightened of a donkey
at all. So he turned and pounced,
tearing the donkey to bits.

False confidence often
leads into danger.

The Donkey
and its
Driver

There was once a donkey that was being driven by its owner along the edge of a high cliff. A sudden noise in the undergrowth scared the donkey, which bolted. Unfortunately, it charged towards the clifftop – and in its fright, it didn't think to stop.

The owner was horrified and chased after the donkey, throwing himself at the beast to stop it going over the edge. The man managed to catch hold of the donkey's tail, and held on for dear life. However, the donkey kept trying so hard to plunge over the cliff that in the end the man was forced to let it go, rather than be pulled over with it.

Don't be too stubborn in wanting your own way.

Jupiter
and the
Tortoise

Long ago in the early days of the
world, the great god Jupiter ruled the
Earth. The time came when he was to marry, and
he was determined to hold a splendid wedding
feast. Jupiter invited not just the other gods
and goddesses but all the animals too. Every
creature was delighted to be asked.

The wedding day arrived, the ceremony was
performed, and then everyone gathered for the
banquet. Jupiter looked around with pride, but
he noticed that one animal was missing – the

tortoise. The feast was a huge success, but Jupiter was disappointed that the tortoise had not turned up, so he went to ask him why.

"I don't care for going out," said the tortoise, "there's no place like home."

Jupiter was enraged by this reply, and declared that from then onwards the tortoise should carry his house on his back, and never be able to get away from home even if he wished to.

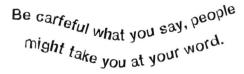

Be carfeful what you say, people might take you at your word.

The Farmer
and the
Fox

There was once a farmer who was
bothered by a fox, which came prowling
around his farmyard every night. Each morning,
the farmer awoke to find yet more of his
chickens, ducks or geese had been carried off.

So the farmer set a trap and caught the fox.
As punishment, he tied a bunch of dry
brushwood to the fox's tail and set fire to it.

The terrified creature ran off, trying to
escape from the fire burning at its tail. However,
the fox began making straight for the farmer's

fields, where
the corn was
standing ripe and
ready for cutting. As
the fox ran through the
corn, it quickly caught fire,
destroying the farmer's harvest.

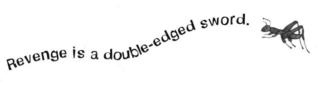

Revenge is a double-edged sword.

The TWO Frogs

There were once two frogs who were neighbours. One lived in a marsh, where there was plenty of water, which frogs love. The other dwelled in a lane some distance away, where there was no water except for the puddles which lay about after it had rained.

The marsh frog often worried about the other frog. She was anxious that if there were several weeks without rain, the puddles would dry up – and so would her neighbour. The marsh frog warned her friend and pressed him to come and live with her in the marsh, for he would find his surroundings there far more comfortable and – more importantly – safe. But the other refused, saying that he could not bring himself to move from a place to which he had become accustomed.

A few days afterwards it rained, and there were lots of puddles in the lane for the frog to splash in. Suddenly, a heavy wagon came down the lane, and the frog was crushed to death beneath the wheels.

Do not fear change, it is often for the better.

The Goatherd
and the
Goat

One day, a goatherd was out on a rocky mountainside where his goats had been grazing. It was time to round them up and take them down to the lowlands for the night. However, one of the goats had strayed off and was refusing to join the rest.

The goatherd tried to get her back by calling and whistling, but the goat took no notice of him. He grew more and more annoyed until at last he lost his temper completely, and picked up a stone and threw it at her. To his horror, he saw

that he had broken one
of her horns.

The goatherd
begged the goat
not to tell his
master, but she
replied, "You silly
boy, my broken horn
will tell what's happened,
even if I hold my tongue."

It's no use trying to hide
what can't be hidden.

The
Astronomer

There was once an astronomer who
enjoyed staying up at night and going out
to watch the stars. The darker it was, the better
it was for seeing the stars. So the man used to
walk outside the town, away from all the lit lamps
in the houses and streets, into the countryside
where there was no light at all. Then he would
make himself comfortable and spend hours
watching the heavens.

One night, the astronomer had made his way
into the fields and was walking along gazing

upwards as usual. He was so absorbed with looking up and not watching where he was going, that he fell into a dry well.

He lay there groaning, and was extremely lucky when a traveller passed by. The traveller came to the edge of the well, looked down, and asked the astronomer what had happened.

But when the astronomer explained, the traveller said, "If you were looking so hard at the sky that you didn't even see where your feet were taking you, it appears to me that you deserve all you've got."

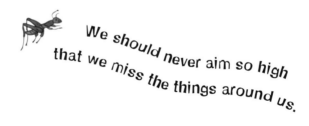

We should never aim so high that we miss the things around us.

The Donkey
and his
Burdens

Once upon a time, there was a pedlar who owned a donkey. One day he went to market and bought as much salt as the donkey could carry to sell in nearby villages. He loaded the donkey with the salt and then set off home to store it there.

On the way, the pedlar and the donkey came to a stream with only a plank of wood across it for a bridge. The pedlar could walk across it easily on his two legs, but the donkey found it very narrow for his four feet. Unfortunately the

donkey stumbled and fell into the water.

The pedlar was much more concerned with the state of the salt than he was with the donkey. Of course, much of the salt drained away in the water. How furious the pedlar was to have lost some of his stock through this mishap.

While this was bad luck for the pedlar, it was good luck for the donkey. When the animal was up on its feet again, it found that the load had become much lighter. It was dismayed when its master drove straight back to market and bought more salt, then started out for home, fully loaded once more.

No sooner had they reached the stream than the donkey deliberately fell off the plank, lay down in the water, and rose as before with a much lighter load. But its master realized the donkey was trying to trick him. He turned back to market once more, bought a large number of sponges, and piled them on the donkey's back.

When they came to the stream, the donkey lay down again. But as the sponges soaked up lots of water, it found that when it stood up, it had an even bigger burden to carry than ever.

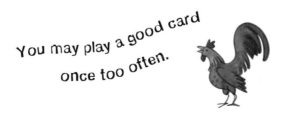

You may play a good card once too often.

3¹⁴

Feathers and Fools

The Fox
and the
Stork

There was once a time when a fox and a stork were good friends. They enjoyed each other's company, chatting about this and that, and often went to visit each other.

Once, the fox invited the stork to dinner. He thought he would play a joke on her. So when it came to serving the meal, he put nothing in front of her except some soup in a very shallow dish. There was nothing else to eat, and no spoon either. The fox could easily lap up his soup with his tongue. But of course the stork had a very long, thin bill, which was no good for lapping up soup. All she could do was dip the end of her bill in the shallow dish. She was very disappointed and left the meal as hungry as when she arrived.

The fox laughed to himself when he saw that the stork had to leave her soup. "I'm sorry," he said, "that the soup is not to your liking."

"Do not apologise," said the stork as she left. "I've had a lovely time and I hope you will come to me for dinner soon." So they fixed a date when the fox would go for dinner at the stork's house.

When the day came, and the pair were seated at the table in the stork's kitchen, the fox saw that the meal was contained in a very long, narrow jar. Even though the fox had quite a long, thin nose, the jar was even longer and thinner. He couldn't reach any of the delicious soup inside. All he could manage to do was to lick the top of

the jar. However, the stork could easily fit her long, thin bill inside.

"I will not apologise," said the stork "because you should do as you would be done by."

Treat others as you would wish to be treated.

The Owl
and the
Birds

There was once an owl, who, in her wisdom, advised the rest of the birds that whenever they noticed a little shoot growing from an acorn, they should pull it up out of the ground. The owl said that acorns encouraged the growth of mistletoe, from which hunters could make sticky bird-lime. The hunters would then paste the bird-lime onto reeds, which they would place in trees, bushes and hedgerows. Then birds would get stuck to the reeds and be caught by the hunters.

The owl also advised the other birds to pluck up the seed of the flax plant, which people often grew as crops. The flax was then used to make nets and snares to trap birds.

Lastly the owl, seeing an archer approach, predicted that this man would make arrows from feathers that fell from the birds, which would be able to fly faster than the wings of the birds themselves. These too would be used to kill birds.

The birds all thought that the owl had gone mad, and took no notice of these warning words. However afterwards, many of them found out the hard way that her words were true. Then they marvelled at her knowledge and decided that she must be the wisest of birds.

But by then it was too late. Now, whenever the birds look up to the owl and ask for her

advice, she no longer
gives it. She just hangs her head and
feels sorry for their earlier stupidity.

Destroy the seed of evil, or it
will grow up to be your ruin.

The Jackdaw
and the
Doves

O nce there was a jackdaw who saw that some doves living in a warm, safe dovecote were provided with food by their owner. The jackdaw wished to share in this easy life and tried to disguise himself as a dove by painting himself white.

The unwitting doves didn't notice and let him into their cote. The crafty jackdaw was careful to be silent, so he wouldn't give himself away by letting the gentle-voiced doves hear his harsh cry. However, the longer he spent with them the more relaxed he became. One day he forgot himself and began to chatter. Horrified, the doves kicked him out at once, pecking him hard.

So the jackdaw returned to his own kind. But because he was white, his friends failed to recognize him. They too turned him away.

So in trying to win favour with two sets of birds, he ended up gaining neither.

If you try to be all things to all people, you may well please no one — not even yourself.

The Lark
and her
Young Ones

Long ago, in early springtime one year, a lark made her nest in the green stalks of some very young wheat. She laid a clutch of tiny eggs and looked after them carefully until they hatched. Then she cared for her brood with the utmost attention until they had almost grown to their full strength. The lark's little ones had grown nearly all their wing feathers, and were almost able to fly, when the owner of the field came to look over his crop — which by now was fully grown and ripe.

"The wheat is ready," he said to himself. "The time has come when I must ask my neighbours to help me with this year's harvest."

One of the young larks heard his words and anxiously hurried to tell his mother. "We can't stay here, Mother," he warned, "it isn't safe. Wherever shall we go?"

"Don't worry, my son," his mother urged. "There is no reason to move quite yet. The man is only going to ask his friends to help him with the harvest, he's not going to do anything straight away."

It was indeed a few days later before the owner of the field came again. By this time, the grain was falling from the wheat because it was becoming over-ripe. "Hmm..." he said. "I really must come myself tomorrow with my men, and with as many other reapers as I can hire, and I will get in the harvest."

The mother lark heard these words herself and said to her brood, "It is time to be off now, my little ones, for the man is in earnest this time — he no longer trusts his friends, but will reap the field himself."

 Depend on yourself more than others.

The Farmer and the Stork

One spring, a farmer and his labourers
worked hard to plough the fields and sow
the seed, doing their best to ensure a good
harvest later in the year. However, no sooner was
all the seed in the ground than a flock of
cranes swooped down and began to peck at it.

The farmer and his men tried everything
they could think of to get rid of the cranes –
from running at the birds while flapping their
arms, to setting up scarecrows – but the
cranes kept coming back. In the end, the

farmer decided to lay nets all over the fields, which would not keep the birds away, but might catch them when they landed.

Sure enough, when the farmer went out to check his fields the next day there was a stork trapped in one of the nets. It was flapping its wings frantically, trying to get free.

"Please spare my life," the stork begged. "I ask you to let me go free this once. I think my leg is broken — please have pity on me. Besides, I know you set these nets to catch cranes. I am not a crane, I am a stork, a bird of excellent character. Look at my feathers — they are not at all like a crane's."

However, the farmer just laughed and said, "It may be all as you say, but I only know this: I have

caught you in the
company of those
robbers the cranes,
and you must die in
their company too."

Birds of a feather
flock together.

The Swan
and the
Raven

A raven once caught sight of a swan and couldn't help but feel jealous at the elegant bird's long neck and snow-white feathers. The raven became eaten up with envy. All he could think of was how he too could get the same beautiful plumage.

'Maybe the swan's clean colour comes from the water in which he swims?' the raven wondered. So he went to soak himself in the swan's lakes and pools. But no matter how many times the raven washed, he didn't

330

become even a
tiny bit white. Instead, he
was bedraggled and hungry, as he
couldn't find any food. In the end, he
returned to his old habitat and had
to be satisfied with his lot.

You can try to change your behaviour
but it won't change what you are.

331

The Eagle
and the
Kite

An eagle once sat in the branches of a tree next to a kite. The lordly bird was sighing and hanging his head in sorrow.

"Whatever is the matter?" asked the kite. "You seem terribly downcast."

"Oh I am," moaned the eagle. "I've looked everywhere for a suitable mate to keep me company and I simply can't find one."

"Why not take me?" replied the kite, without hesitating. "I would be a good match for you. In fact, I am much stronger than you."

"Ah, but are you able to live on what you hunt and catch, like I do?" quizzed the eagle.

The kite shrugged. "Well, I have often caught and carried away a full-grown ostrich in my talons," she insisted.

The eagle was impressed by these words. 'An ostrich,' he thought. 'This kite must be strong and important indeed.' He didn't need any more thought but accepted the kite's offer and took her as his mate.

The couple were soon married and held a fine wedding to which all the other birds were invited. Everyone celebrated. Then the eagle and the kite began the daily business of living together. One day the eagle said to his new wife, "Why don't you fly off and bring me back the ostrich you promised me."

The kite instantly soared aloft into the air – but when she returned, all she brought back was a straggly mouse, stinking from the length of time it had lain in the fields.

The eagle wrinkled up his beak in disgust. "Is this," he said, "the faithful fulfilment of your promise to me?"

The kite replied with a smirk, "In order to obtain your royal hand in marriage, there is nothing that I would not have promised."

Do not trust everything people say.

The Eagle and the Jackdaw

A majestic eagle was once perched high up on a lofty rock, from where he could look down on the world beneath him.

Suddenly, something small and white caught his eye, moving far below. At once, he launched himself off the rock and swooped down, seizing a lamb and carrying it off in his talons.

A jackdaw had been standing near the lamb, and this took him quite by surprise. He was full of admiration for the mighty eagle and wished with all his heart that he could be as strong and swift. So he decided to give it a go. He flew around with a great whir of his wings and settled upon a large ram, intending to carry him off. But his claws became entangled in the ram's fleece and he was not able to get himself free, even though he fluttered with his wings as much as he could.

The shepherd was nearby and saw what had happened. He at once ran over and seized the jackdaw. Once he had cut him free from the ram's wool, he clipped his wings so he could no longer fly. That evening he took him home and gave him to his children as a pet.

The children were delighted and quizzed their father, saying, "Wherever did you find it? And what sort of a bird is it?"

He replied, "To my knowledge it is a jackdaw, but it would like you to think it is an eagle."

If you pretend to be something you are not, prepare to be found out.

The Rooster
and the
Pearl

Once upon a time, a proud rooster was strutting up and down the farmyard among the hens when he suddenly spied something shining in the straw. "Ho! Ho!" said the rooster. "Whatever it is, it's for me."

He looked all around to check that no one was watching him, then he scratched and pecked, and rooted the object out from beneath the straw. It turned out to be a pearl that had somehow had been lost in the yard.

Although it was clearly very beautiful, the

rooster was mightily disappointed. "To humans, you may be a treasure," he sighed. "But for me, I would much rather have a single barleycorn to eat than a whole string of pearls, for they are of no use to me."

Precious things are for those that can prize them.

The Eagle and the Fox

Long ago, there lived an eagle and a fox who struck up a friendship and decided to live near each other. The eagle built her nest in a tall tree, and hatched a brood of chicks, while the fox crept into the undergrowth and produced her young there.

Not long after they had agreed upon this plan, the eagle failed to find any food for her chicks for

several days.
Eventually the eagle
couldn't listen to their starving cries any longer.
Seeing that the fox had gone out hunting, she
swooped down, seized one of the young cubs
and carried it back up to her nest, where she
fed it to her own babies.

When the fox returned she knew at once
what had happened. She was grief-stricken,
horrified and furious — and frustrated that she
could do nothing to punish the eagle.
However, a punishment soon
fell on the eagle of its own doing.

Not long afterwards, the eagle was hovering near a fire on which some villagers were cooking a goat, when she seized a piece of the flesh, and carried it to her nest. She did not realize that a burning cinder was attached to the piece of meat. A strong breeze soon fanned the spark into a flame, and the eaglets, as yet with no wing feathers and therefore totally helpless, were roasted in their nest. The dead eaglets dropped at the foot of the tree, where the fox and her young made a tasty meal of them.

What goes around comes around.

The Hawk and the Nightingale

A nightingale was once sitting high up in an oak tree, singing beautifully, when she was seen by a hawk who was out hunting. The hawk swooped down and seized the nightingale, who begged him to spare her life.

"Please sir, let me go," the nightingale trilled. "Surely I am not big enough to satisfy the hunger of such a mighty creature as yourself. If you are in need of a decent meal, you would be better off capturing much bigger birds than I, or even small creatures that live in the field."

However, the hawk interrupted her, saying, "I should indeed have lost my senses if I should let go of food ready in my hand, for the sake of pursuing food that I have not laid eyes on yet."

A bird in the hand is worth two in the bush.

The Hawk, the Kite and the Pigeons

A flock of pigeons were once terrified by the appearance of a kite in the sky. They called for the nearest fighting bird for help – which happened to be a hawk. The hawk agreed, and soared off to deal with the kite.

However, when the hawk returned, he killed more of the pigeons in a few minutes than the kite could have killed in a year.

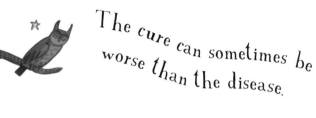

The cure can sometimes be worse than the disease.

The Peacock and the Crane

There was once a conceited peacock who had a beautiful tail. One day, he met a crane, and began to mock his grey plumage.

"Look at my feathers," boasted the peacock. "See how bright they are. Yours are so dull!"

"That may be true," the crane replied, "but I can fly high in the sky, from where I can see the beauty of the Earth. Whereas you just strut around on the ground like a common creature."

Fine feathers don't make fine birds.

The Cat
and the
Cockerel

A cat was slinking about in the fields one day when he caught a special treat – a cockerel. The cat began to think how he could justify killing and eating the cockerel.

"People would thank me for getting rid of you," he yowled, "because you crow at night and keep everyone awake."

"But Mr Cat, that's not true – people think I'm useful," the cockerel blustered, "for I do it to help everyone get up in time to go to work."

Then the cat gave a shrug and said, "Well, no matter. Whatever you say, I'm not going to go without supper." And he made a meal of him.

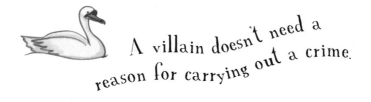

A villain doesn't need a reason for carrying out a crime.

The Fighting Birds and the Eagle

One day, on a certain farm, two cockerels were fighting each other to prove who was the strongest, and earn the right to be master of the farmyard. Both fought bravely, and for a long time they seemed to be equally matched, but at last one was victorious. The beaten cockerel skulked away and hid himself in a quiet corner, while the conqueror, flying up to a wall, flapped his wings and crowed boastfully with all his might.

However at that very moment, an eagle

came sailing through the air and pounced
upon the winner, and carried him off in his
talons. The losing cockerel immediately came
out of his corner, and from then on ruled over
the whole farmyard completely unchallenged.

Pride comes before a fall.

The Bird-catcher, the Partridge and the Rooster

There was once a bird-catcher who had spent the entire day out in the fields but had failed to catch anything in his traps.

He was about to sit down to a dinner of vegetables when a friend unexpectedly came visiting. The bird-catcher felt obliged to offer his friend some food — but the only meat he had was a partridge, which he had tamed to use as bait when he went hunting. Nevertheless the bird-catcher prepared to kill the partridge, until he heard it beg, "What will you do without me? Who will lure the birds to your nets? And besides, who will chirp you to sleep at night?"

The bird-catcher thought for an instant and decided to spare the partridge's life after all. Instead, he decided to kill a young cockerel in the yard outside, which would just about make a meal. But the cockerel cried out, "If you kill me, who will wake you every day at dawn?"

The bird-catcher replied, "It's true, you are an excellent bird, but my friend and I must have our dinner."

People in need don't follow reason or rules.

The Crow
and Mercury

A long time ago, a crow became caught in a snare. He prayed to the great god Apollo to release him, and he vowed that if the god did indeed help him, he would pray and make a special offering at the god's shrine.

Apollo heard the creature's desperate cries and came to his rescue – the crow suddenly found that the snare snapped open, releasing his leg. The crow was overjoyed.

However, the minute he hopped away and took to the skies, he totally forgot his promise.

He went nowhere near Apollo's shrine but hurried straight back to his family and friends. Shortly afterwards, the crow again became caught in a snare. He didn't dare to ask Apollo for help once more, so instead he offered up the same promise to the god Mercury. But the crow was not so lucky a second time. Mercury suddenly appeared before

him and said, "Do you take me for a fool? How can I believe your vows, when you have clearly lied to my friend?"

Always keep your promises.

The Eagle
and the
Arrow

Once upon a time, a
mighty eagle was soaring
through the air, strong and powerful.
Suddenly it heard the whizz of a speeding
arrow, and felt itself pierced in the heart.

The eagle looked down and saw
that it was indeed badly wounded,
with blood pouring from its breast.
Slowly the bird fluttered down to the
ground, where it lay dying.

Looking down upon the arrow with which it

had been pierced, the eagle's last thought was the realization that the shaft of the arrow had been feathered with one of its own plumes.

We often give our enemies the means for our own destruction.

357

The Fighting Birds and the Partridge

A man who kept poultry once had two fighting cockerels among his birds. One day, by chance, he found a tame partridge for sale. He bought it and brought it home to be reared with the fighting cockerels. However, when the partridge was put into the poultry yard, the cockerels flew at it and followed it about, and the partridge became distressed.

Of course, the partridge thought that the game birds were treating him so badly because he was a stranger. Yet not long afterwards he

saw them fighting each other. They fought furiously, and did not quit until one had well and truly beaten the other. Then the partridge said to himself, "I won't get upset anymore at being bullied by these birds, for they can't even stop quarrelling with each other."

Strangers should avoid those who quarrel among themselves.

The Crow
and the
Serpent

There was once a crow who was starving. He used what little energy he had left to set out on one last flight to find food. Imagine how relieved he was when he noticed a serpent asleep in a sunny nook. Swooping down, the crow seized it greedily.

The serpent was not about to die without a fight. It suddenly darted forward, biting the crow with a mortal wound.

The crow died in agony from the poison, saying, "Oh unhappy me! I thought I had got lucky but in fact I had discovered my own downfall!"

What seems to be a blessing is not always the case.

The Eagle and his Captor

A mighty eagle was once captured by a man, who immediately clipped its wings so it could no longer fly. As if this wasn't enough humiliation, the man then put the eagle – Lord of the Birds – into his poultry yard with all the common chickens, turkeys and geese. Of course, at this, the eagle was weighed down with grief.

Some time later, the man's neighbour bought the eagle for a large sum of money. This man allowed the eagle's feathers to grow again and then set it free.

The eagle couldn't believe the man's kindness. Overjoyed to be flying, it soared into the skies. Then it swooped back down and caught a hare, taking it to the man as a gift.

A passing fox saw what the eagle had done and couldn't believe it. "What are you doing trying to please this man?" he exclaimed. "You should be trying to win the favour of your former owner. You never know, he may hunt for you again and clip your wings a second time."

Keep your friends close but your enemies closer.

Heroes and Villains

365

The Crow
and the
Sheep

A sheep was once grazing in a field, minding her own business, when a large crow flapped down and seated himself on her back. The sheep was rather annoyed but decided to ignore it. She ambled back and forth, from one patch of sweet grass to the next, with the crow admiring the view from his high perch.

The sheep carried the crow back and forth for a long time against her will, and at last said, "If you had treated a dog in this way, you would quickly have been punished by his sharp teeth."

To this the crow replied, "I despise the weak but of course I give way to the strong. I know whom I may bully and whom I must flatter, and this is how I am going to stay alive to reach a grand old age."

Self-serving people treat the weak with contempt and the strong with respect.

The Wolf and the Crane

There was once a hungry wolf who was out hunting and came across a young deer. He gave chase, killed it and began feasting on it, delighted with his delicious meal.

Suddenly, he felt something stick in his throat and he realized it must be a small bone. He tried swallowing hard, but it wouldn't go down. Then he coughed and coughed, but the bone wouldn't come up. All this time his throat was becoming sore and he was getting agitated. After a while, the soreness was unbearable. The

wolf ran up and down groaning and looking for something to relieve the pain.

Desperately, the wolf sought out other creatures to help him and begged them to try to remove the bone. "I would give anything," he gasped to them, "if you would take it out." But of course most creatures were afraid of the wolf and would have nothing to do with him.

At last the crane agreed to try. The brave bird told the wolf to open his jaws as wide as he could. Then, trying not to think of the sharp teeth, the crane put her long neck down the wolf's throat, and with her beak loosened the bone until it came out. The wolf was hugely relieved and leapt about for joy.

"Now, will you kindly give me the reward you promised?" asked the crane.

The wolf grinned and showed his teeth again, saying, "Be content. You have put your head inside a wolf's mouth and taken it out again in safety. That should be reward enough for you."

Gratitude and greed do not go together.

The
Sick Lion

Once upon a time there lived an old lion who was famous for his strength and courage. He had performed amazing feats and truly earned the title King of the Beasts.

However, now he had fallen very sick and he knew it was almost his time to die. He went to lie at the mouth of his cave, looking out over his kingdom. Then all the other animals came round him and drew nearer as he became more helpless. However, when they saw him on the point of death, they said to each other, "Now is the time to pay off old grudges." So the boar came and drove at the lion with his tusks. Then a bull gored him with his horns. When the animals saw that the lion didn't have the strength to do anything, even the donkey, feeling quite safe, came up. Turning his tail to the lion, he kicked his heels into him as hard as he could.

"This is a double death," growled the lion. "I am not just weak and helpless, but I have to suffer being tormented by animals who would never dare come near me otherwise."

Only cowards insult dying majesty.

Androcles
and the
Lion

In ancient days long gone by, there was once a slave named Androcles who was forced to work under a very cruel master. One day he took his chance and managed to escape from his master's house, fleeing to the surrounding forest. Androcles was of course overjoyed to be free, but now he had new troubles. What was he to do next? Where was he to go? How was he to live?

He wandered through the forest, pondering these questions, when he came upon a mighty lion groaning with pain. Androcles' first thought was to run for his life. But then he stood, curious as to why the lion didn't spring up and pounce. After a while, when the lion had continued to groan, but not move at all, Androcles cautiously went closer... and closer... and closer... until he was near enough to touch the lion.

Then the great beast stretched out its paw, and Androcles saw that it was swollen and bleeding. Full of pity, and forgetting his fear, he bent to examine it. He discovered that a huge thorn was stuck in it, which was causing the pain. He delicately pulled out the thorn and bound up the lion's paw. The lion bowed its mighty head to Androcles and rubbed its mane against him, and even licked his hand.

Androcles followed the lion to its cave and took shelter there. The great beast then bounded off to hunt for meat for Androcles to eat, and this is how they lived from then on – until one day, when hunters came to that part of the forest. Androcles and the lion tried to flee, but they were outnumbered and the hunters caught them, and dragged them both off to the city. The lion was taken away to fight in front of huge crowds at the arena, for in those days people thought it was sport to see men and animals fight to the death.

Meanwhile, Androcles was put on trial for escaping from his master's house. His punishment was death – by being thrown to a lion in the arena.

The day arrived when fighting in the arena was to take place. Everyone in the city came to see the spectacle, ruled over by the emperor and his court. After several men had fought each other before the roaring crowd, Androcles was led out to the centre of the sandy arena. He stood in terror, fearing the worst. Then a lion was let loose from a dungeon beneath the arena and came bounding towards Androcles.

But as soon as the lion came near to Androcles it stopped and bowed its head, licking his hands. It was the lion from the forest – Androcles' friend.

Everyone was astounded, and the emperor summoned Androcles to him, who told the whole story. After hearing this, the emperor told Androcles that he was pardoned and free to go,

and the lion was also let loose to return to its home in the forest.

Gratitude is the sign of noble souls.

The Woodman and the Serpent

Once upon a time, there was a woodman who had been hard at work all day, chopping logs in the snow. At last it was time to go home.

As he tramped through the forest, he noticed something black lying on the ground ahead. When he came closer, he saw that it was a serpent. It looked frozen with cold. The woodman took pity on the creature, and just in case there was some hope of reviving it, he picked it up and put it in his jacket to warm it.

As soon as the woodman got indoors he put

the serpent down before the fire. His children were curious and kept close watch. To their surprise, they suddenly saw the serpent's tail twitch. Its eyes opened. Then it wriggled. Then it flicked out its forked tongue. The children were delighted and one of them tried to stroke it. But the serpent raised its head and went to bite the child. Just in time, the woodman seized his axe and with one stroke cut the serpent in two.

Don't expect gratitude from the wicked.

The Ant and the Dove

Once upon a time, a thirsty ant went to the stream for a drink. However, as the ant reached down to take a sip, it fell in, and was carried away by the rushing water.

The poor little ant was on the point of drowning when a dove, sitting on a tree overhanging the water, plucked a leaf and let it fall into the stream. The ant used the last of its strength to scramble on to it, then floated safely to the bank, exhausted but alive.

Soon afterwards, a bird-catcher came along

and saw the dove
sitting in the tree. Unnoticed by the dove, he
set a trap for her. But the tiny ant saw what he
had done. It raced up to the bird-catcher and
bit him as hard as it could. The bird-catcher
cried out, and the noise startled the dove,
who flew off, safe and free.

The grateful heart will always find
opportunities to show its gratitude.

381

The Nurse
and the
Wolf

There was once a nurse who was looking after a little child who kept crying. "Be quiet now," she said, holding the child, "if you make that noise again I will give you to the wolf."

Now it chanced that a wolf was passing under the window and heard the nurse saying this. So he crouched down by the house and waited.

'I am in luck today,' he thought. 'The child is sure to cry again soon, then the nurse will throw it out for me to grab. And a daintier morsel I haven't had for many a day.'

So the wolf waited and waited, until at last he heard the child crying again. The wolf sat under the window and looked up to the nurse, wagging his tail. But all the nurse did was gasp in horror and slam the window shut. She shrieked, calling for help, and the dogs of the house came bounding out, snarling.

Then the wolf realized that the nurse hadn't meant what she said, and he fled for his life, his tail between his legs.

Enemies' promises were made to be broken.

The Cat
and the
Birds

There once lived a cat who heard that the birds living in a nearby aviary had fallen ill. The cat decided that this would be the ideal opportunity for him to catch them. So he disguised himself as a doctor and set off for the aviary.

Once there, the cat presented himself at the door, and enquired after the health of the birds.

"We shall be much better," they replied, without letting him in, "when we have seen the last of you."

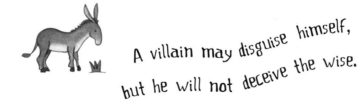

A villain may disguise himself, but he will not deceive the wise.

The Old Hound

There was once a hound that had served its master well for many years. When they had been out hunting together, the hunt had been plentiful every time. However, now the hound was growing old and it had begun to lose its strength and speed, as well as most of its teeth.

One day, when out hunting, the hound's master startled a wild boar.

The boar set off at a pace and the man set the hound after it. The hound ran as fast as it could and caught up with the boar, and seized it by the ear. But as the hound had hardly any teeth, it could not keep a grip.
The boar managed to wrench free and escape.

The man began to scold his dog, but the hound interrupted him with these words, "My will is as strong as ever, but my body is old and feeble. You ought to honour me for what I have been instead of abusing me for what I am now."

Respect your elders.

The Two Soldiers and the Robber

There were once two soldiers travelling together on a road when they were set upon by a robber. One of the soldiers took to his heels and ran away. However, the other stood his ground and drew his sword. He put up such a fight that the robber was forced to flee and leave him in peace.

When the coast was clear, the first soldier returned, brandishing his weapon and crying in a loud voice, "Where is he? Let me at him, I'll soon let him know who he has to deal with."

The brave soldier stood gasping for breath after his fight, and replied, "You are a little late, my friend. I only wish you had backed me up just now, even if you had done no more than shout and wave your sword about. Calm yourself, and put away your weapon – there is no further use for it. You may delude others into thinking you're as brave as a lion, but I know that at the first sign of danger, you run away like a hare."

It is no good pretending to be brave after the event.

The Blind Man and the Cub

There was once a blind man who had so fine a sense of touch that when any animal was put into his hands, he could tell exactly what it was merely by feeling it. He could tell a mole from its velvety coat. He could tell a lizard from its scaly skin. He could tell a chick from its fluffy down and a goose from its long feathers.

One day, a wolf cub was placed in his hands, and he was asked what he thought it was. He felt the cub all over for some time, and then said, "Indeed, I am not sure whether it is a wolf's cub or

391

a fox's, but this I do know — it would never do to trust it in a herd of sheep."

Evil tendencies are early shown.

The
Quack Frog

Once upon a time, a frog lived deep in the marshes, where no one ever came to see him. He felt unloved and quite alone. 'How can I make myself important to others,' he wondered, 'so that they want to see me and talk to me?'

The frog thought hard and hit upon an idea. He dressed himself as a doctor and practised putting on a wise expression, and talking in a clever way. Then he left his home in the marshes and went off into the world, proclaiming to be a learned doctor, knowledgeable about medicines

and able to cure diseases.

Creatures came from far and wide to see if he could cure their illnesses. But among the crowd was a fox, who called out, "You, a doctor! How can you claim to heal others when you cannot even cure your own bent legs and blotched and wrinkled skin?"

Those who say they can heal others should first heal themselves, then they may be believed.

The Wolf
and the
Sheep

Once upon a time, a wolf was set upon by a pack of angry dogs. He was bitten and torn, then left for dead.

However after some time, the wolf began to feel strength returning to his limbs. When he managed to raise his head, he saw a sheep passing by and cried out for help.

"Please my friend sheep, would you kindly bring me some water from the stream close by? I think I could just about manage to get up and find meat, if only I could get something to drink."

But this sheep was no fool. "I can understand," she said, "that if I brought you the water, you would have no difficulty about finding the meat. Good morning." And she escaped while she could.

Being careful is sometimes better than being brave.

The Lion
and the
Bull

A **long time ago,** a bull lived among a herd of cattle in a field of lush grass. He grew fine and fat through grazing and living an easy life.

One day a lion passed by the field. When he saw the cattle his mouth began to water – but when he spied the huge bull he began to drool. The lion went away and thought hard about how he could get the bull in his clutches.

After a while he hit upon an idea, and sent the bull an invitation to come to dinner. The bull was flattered at being asked to dine with the

King of the Beasts and of course he accepted at once. He boasted to all the cattle in the field about his important appointment and made sure that his coat was free of mud and his hooves and horns were shining.

That evening, at the appointed hour, the excited bull made his way to the lion's den. The lion welcomed him and told the bull to come in and make himself at home. However, the bull noticed that although he saw a great array of saucepans, roasting spits and other kitchen equipment, there was little sign of anything cooking other than soup.

The bull was clever and his suspicions were immediately aroused. Without giving it a second thought, he turned on his heels and walked away. The lion called after him in a hurt tone to ask the reason why, and the bull turned around and said,

"I have reason enough. When I saw all your preparations it struck me at once that dinner was to be a bull."

If you lay your plans in front of your enemies you will fail.

The Wolf
and the
Shepherd

A shepherd was out on the hillside one day when he heard a yelping noise like a puppy. He was surprised to find a tiny wolf cub. The shepherd could not think of leaving the tiny creature there, so he took it home.

The shepherd reared the cub with his dogs, training it to herd the sheep this way and that. When the cub grew to his full size, if ever a wolf stole a sheep from the flock, it would join the dogs in hunting it down. If the dogs failed to find the thief, the wolf would continue the hunt alone, and when it found the culprit, would stop and share the feast. As well as this, if some time passed without a sheep being carried off by the wolves, it would steal one itself.

Eventually, the shepherd became suspicious. So he kept a close watch on the wolf, until he caught it in the act of stealing a sheep. And that was the end of the ungrateful creature.

What's bred in the bone is sure to come out in the flesh.

The Farmer
and the
Viper

One day, a farmer was out in his fields sowing
seeds when he found a viper lying
motionless on the soil. The farmer looked closely
and thought that although the viper was either
very ill or injured, there was some life left in it yet.
So he kindly picked it up and tucked it inside his
jacket – he hoped that the warmth of his body
might revive it.

Colour did indeed begin to return to the
viper's skin, and it gradually began to awaken and
move. No sooner did the viper realize where it

was than it turned upon the kind farmer and sunk its poisonous fangs into him.

"It's my own fault," groaned the farmer as he lay dying. "I should have known better than to show kindness to such a wicked creature."

Kindness is thrown away upon the evil.

The Soldier
and his
Horse

It was wartime, and a soldier looked after his horse with great care. He gave it a plentiful supply of oats and water, and groomed and exercised it every day, for he wished the horse to be strong enough to endure the hardships of the battlefield.

However when the war was over, the soldier completely changed his habits. He made the horse do all sorts of hard tasks, such as drawing carts and carrying heavy packs. He gave it only chaff to eat and hardly ever brushed its coat or checked its hooves.

The time came when war broke out again. Once more, the soldier saddled his horse for battle. He put on his heavy uniform along with his pack and weapons, then mounted his horse. But the half-starved beast sank under his weight.

"You will have to go to battle on foot this time," said the horse. "Due to hard work and bad food, you have turned me into a donkey, and you cannot in a moment turn me into a horse again."

When you have something that is of value, always look after it properly.

The Donkey and the Wolf

There was **once a donkey** who was feeding in a meadow. To his horror, he caught sight of his enemy the wolf approaching in the distance, and knew he would be eaten unless he came up with a plan. So the donkey suddenly pretended to be very lame and hobbled painfully along. When the wolf reached him, he asked the donkey how he came to be so lame.

"I went through a hedge and trod on a thorn," said the donkey. "Please would you pull the offending thorn out with your teeth dear

wolf? Just in case, when you eat me, it should stick in your throat and hurt you very much."

"How thoughtful of you," snarled the wolf, and said that of course he would help. He told the donkey to lift up his foot, and set his mind to getting out the thorn.

But the donkey suddenly kicked out with his heels and gave the wolf a blow to the mouth, breaking his teeth. He then galloped off at full speed.

As soon as he was able, the wolf growled to himself, "It serves me right. My father taught me to kill, and I should have stuck to that trade instead of attempting to cure."

Everyone has his trade and should stick to it.

The Wolves and the Dogs

Once upon a time, the wolves said to the dogs, "Why should we continue to be enemies any longer? You are like us in many ways, the main difference between us is only that of training. We live a life of freedom, but you are people's slaves – they beat you, and put heavy collars around your necks, and make you keep watch over their flocks and herds. To top it off, they give you nothing but bones to eat." The dogs hung their heads in shame and mumbled in agreement.

The wolves continued, "We don't think you should put up with it any longer. Hand over the flocks to us, and we will all live on the fat of the land and feast together."

The dogs thought this sounded like a good plan. The wolves' clever words had persuaded them, and they went off with the wolves to their den. But no sooner were they inside than the wolves set upon them and tore them to pieces.

Traitors richly deserve their fate.

The Athenian
and the
Theban

A man from the city of Athens and a man
from the city of Thebes were once
travelling together. They passed the time in
conversation, as is the way of travellers. After
discussing a variety of subjects they began to
talk about the heroes of old – mighty men who
were half-gods, who had performed incredible
feats of strength and bravery. Each traveller was
full of praise for the heroes of his own city.

Eventually, the man from Thebes claimed
that the famous Hercules was the greatest hero

who had ever lived on Earth, and now occupied a foremost place among the gods. Hercules was a mighty warrior who had killed an enormous lion, beaten a many-headed dragon, captured a giant bull, and stolen a three-headed dog that guarded the gates of hell, among other feats.

At this, the man from Athens insisted that the hero Theseus was far superior, and began to explain why. Theseus, he said, was more intelligent than Hercules. After all, he had used his wits to enter a complicated underground maze called a labyrinth and slay a bull-headed monster called the Minotaur that lived there.

The man from Athens was very good at arguing, and as the man from Thebes was no match for him, he eventually had to give in. "All right, have it your way," he cried. "I only hope that when our heroes are angry with us, Athens

may suffer from the fury of Hercules, and Thebes from the wrath of Theseus."

Brains may beat brawn.

The Key to Happiness

The Crow
and the
Pitcher

There **was once a crow** who had been unable to find water for many days – not even a drop. He was half-dead with thirst, and barely had the energy to hop along the ground. Imagine his amazement and joy when he suddenly came upon a water pitcher.

However, when the crow put its beak into the mouth of the pitcher he found that very little water was left and that he could not reach far enough down to get at it. He tried and tried, but at last had to give up in despair.

The crow knew that he had no energy to go further in search of water, and death must surely be near. A sudden thought occurred to him, and he took a pebble and dropped it into the pitcher. Then he took another pebble and dropped it in. Then another, and another...

At last, he saw the water rise up near him, and after casting in a few more pebbles he was able to quench his thirst and save his life.

Little by little does the trick.

The Town Mouse and the Country Mouse

Once upon a time, a town mouse went on a visit to his cousin in the country. He arrived at the country mouse's home to find that it was a barn, shared with other animals. The country mouse was delighted to see his relative, whom he loved very much, and made the town mouse heartily welcome. The country mouse

418

was poor and lived a simple life. He was also quite rough and ready with his manners and habits. Beans and bacon, cheese and bread, and a bed of straw were all he had to offer the town mouse.

However the town mouse was used to living the high life in the city. He was accustomed to dining on much finer delicacies and sleeping in a much softer bed. He turned his nose up at this country fare and sleeping accommodation.

"I cannot understand," he said to his country cousin, "how you can put up with such poor food, and sleeping on straw with farm creatures nearby. Come home with me and I'll show you how to live. When you have been in town a week you will wonder how you ever lived out here."

The country mouse was curious — after all, he had never seen the town and wondered what it would be like. So, the two mice set off together.

They arrived at the town mouse's residence late at night. It was a grand house, several storeys high, with steps up to a big front door and down to a large cellar. As soon as the mice had squeezed into the cellar through a tiny hole in the bricks, the town mouse took his cousin into a splendid dining room. There, they found the remains of a fine feast on the table, and were soon eating jellies and cakes and all that was nice.

Suddenly the mice heard growling. "What is that?" asked the country mouse.

"It is only the dogs of the house," answered the town mouse in a calm voice.

"Only the dogs!" gasped the country mouse. "I do not like that kind of music at my dinner."

At that moment the door flew open, and in

came two huge dogs. The two terrified mice had to scamper down the table leg and run off.

"Goodbye, cousin," said the country mouse.

"What! Going so soon?" asked the town mouse in surprise.

"Yes," he replied. "Better beans and bacon in peace than cakes and ale in fear."

Better to live poorly in peace than richly in fear.

The Lark Burying her Father

According to ancient legend, the lark was created before the Earth even existed. One day, the lark's father sadly died. But now the little lark was faced with a dilemma – as there was no Earth, where could she bury her father?

The lark had little choice but to let her father's body lie for five days. On the sixth day, not knowing what else to do, she buried him in her own head.

It is said that the gods were very moved by the lark's great efforts to give her father's body a safe resting place. So they rewarded her by adorning her head with a crest, which is often said to be her father's gravestone.

Youth's first duty is reverence to parents.

The Peacock
and
Hera

A **long, long time ago,** in the early days of the world, the gods and goddesses of Mount Olympus ruled over earth, sky and sea. There was once a peacock who prayed earnestly to the goddess Hera, Queen of Mount Olympus. The peacock was more than happy with his beautiful looks, which all the other birds envied, but he longed to have a better singing voice to go with it. He had quite an ugly cry, and what he really wanted was the voice of a nightingale.

However, the great Hera refused. The peacock would not take no for an answer and continued to beg. "Please grant me this," he pleaded, "after all, I am your favourite bird."

But Hera just replied, "Be content with what you have."

 One cannot be first in everything.

The Dog and the Wolf

There was once a wolf who had been cast out from his pack. He hadn't had much luck hunting on his own, and was starving. The wolf had become so thin, his bones were visible beneath his scruffy coat. He was almost dead with hunger when he passed by a dog.

"Ah, cousin," said the dog. "I knew your thieving life would be the ruin of you. Look at me — I guard my master's house, and so I live happily, with food regularly given to me."

Full of pity, the dog suggested, "Come with

me to my master and you shall share my work."

So the wolf and the dog headed towards the town. On the way, the wolf noticed that the hair on a part of the dog's neck was very much worn away, so he asked him how that had happened.

"Oh, it is nothing," said the dog. "That is the place where the collar is put on at night to keep me chained up. It chafes a bit, but you soon get used to it."

"Is that all?" said the wolf. "Then goodbye to you, Master Dog."

Better starve free than be a fat slave.

The Hares
and the
Frogs

There was once a time when the hares were disliked by all the other creatures. They made the hares' lives a misery by taunting and bullying them. The poor hares did not know what to do or where to go to escape from being tormented. Whenever the hares saw another animal approach them, off they would run.

One day a troop of wild horses came stampeding about by the hares, quite on purpose. In a total panic, the hares ran away, but the horses just followed, thundering about with their crashing hooves.

The hares spent hours trying to escape, but to no avail — the horses would not give up. In the end, the despairing hares scuttled off to a nearby lake. They thought it was better to throw themselves in and drown rather than live in fear of being crushed to death by the horses.

But just as the hares got near the bank of the lake, a troop of frogs became frightened of them and scuttled off, jumping into the water.

"Truly," said one of the hares, "things are not as bad as they seem."

There is always someone worse off than yourself.

The Bundle of Sticks

There was once an old man who had several sons. When he knew that his time to die was near, he gathered all his sons together to give them some parting advice.

The man ordered his servants to bring in a bundle of sticks, and then he said to his eldest son, "See if you can break this." The son strained and strained, but with all his efforts was unable to break the bundle.

Then the old man asked another son to try... and another... and another... They all did their

432

utmost, but none of them were successful. "Now untie the sticks," said the father, and the sons did so. He instructed each of them to take a single stick. When they had done so, the dying man called out to them, "Now, try and break them." This time, the sons could all break what was in their hands with hardly any effort at all. "Now you see my meaning," said their father, glad he had left his sons with a gift of wisdom.

Strength lies in united numbers.

433

The Boy
and the
Nettle

A **little boy was once stung** by a nettle. He ran
home crying to his mother and said, "It really
hurts me even though I only touched it gently."

"Ah, that is why," said the boy's mother,
soothingly. "If you touch a nettle again, grasp it
boldly, and it will be gentle to your hand, and
not hurt you in the least."

Whatever you do, do with all your might.

The Fox
and the
Mosquitoes

There **was once a fox** who tried to cross a river and was nearly swept away. He swam for his life and managed to grab a low-hanging branch with his jaws, to drag himself to shore. But as he hauled himself onto the bank, his tail became tangled in a bush and he couldn't move.

A number of mosquitoes saw that the fox was trapped and came and settled on him. They began feasting on him, biting and sucking his blood, and the fox could do nothing at all to get away from their attack.

After a while, a hedgehog came strolling by. He took pity on the fox, and approaching him said, "You are in a very bad way, neighbour. Shall I relieve you by driving off those mosquitoes who are sucking your blood?"

"Thank you, Master Hedgehog," said the fox, "but I would rather you didn't. Please leave them all just where they are."

"Why, how is that?" asked the hedgehog.

"Well, you see," replied the fox, "these mosquitoes have been here a while and have had their fill. If you drive them away, others will come with fresh appetites and bleed me to death."

It's better to choose the lesser of two evils.

The Horse
and the
Mule

There was once a horse and a mule whose owners were travelling down a road. The horse belonged to a knight, and pranced along proudly. However, the mule belonged to a peasant. It plodded along, laden down with a bundle of firewood on its back. "I wish I were you," sighed the mule to the horse, "well fed

438

and groomed, and with splendid harnessing."

At the end of the day, it was time for the peasant and the knight to part company. The mule enviously watched the horse strut away.

Little did the mule know that the horse was off to war. The next day, the horse had to carry the knight into a great battle. The fighting was ruthless, and the horse was in the thick of it. In the final charge, the horse was badly wounded, and left lying in agony among the dead.

Soon afterwards, the mule was led past. He

looked in horror at the remains of the battle and was shocked to see the horse on the point of death. "I was wrong," gasped the mule. "Better humble safety than this fancy danger."

Better to be lowly and safe than important and in danger.

The Farmer
and
Fortune

Once upon a time, a farmer was out ploughing his fields. All at once, his plough hit something solid, which would not budge. The farmer had to stop his horses and fetch a shovel to dig up whatever was in the way.

To his huge surprise, he dug up a pot of golden coins! Of course, he was overjoyed at his discovery. From then on, every day he went to pray at the shrine of the Goddess of the Earth, to say thank you for his find. However, the Goddess of Fortune came to hear about this and was jealous.

She came to see the farmer and angrily demanded, "My man, why do you give Earth the credit for the gift that I gave to you? You have not once thought of thanking me for your good luck! However, should you be unlucky enough to lose what you have gained, I know very well that you would blame me, Fortune, for your bad luck."

Show gratitude where gratitude is due.

The Archer
and the
Tiger

There was once an archer who took his bow and went up into the hills, hoping for a good hunt. Whenever an animal saw him, it fled, terrified — all except a certain tiger. This tiger strode boldly towards the archer and challenged him to fight. But the archer just drew an arrow from his quiver, set it in his bow, and shot it straight into the tiger's flank.

"There!" cried the archer. "You see what my messenger can do? Just you wait a moment and I'll tackle you myself."

The tiger, however, ran away as fast as his legs could carry him, howling in pain.

A fox, who had seen it all happen, said to the tiger, "Come, don't be a coward. Why don't you stay and fight?"

But the tiger said, "You won't get me to stay. If he sends a messenger like that before him, he himself must be a terrible fellow to deal with."

To stay safe, give a wide berth to those who can do damage at a distance.

Jupiter
and the
Monkey

Long, long ago, when the world was new, the
gods and goddesses of Mount Olympus ruled
over everything. Once, the great god Jupiter
who ruled over the Earth issued a proclamation
to all the beasts. He offered a prize to the one
who, in his judgment, produced the most
beautiful offspring.

All the animals were so proud of their children
that they were sure they would win the prize for
themselves. They came in herds and flocks and
swarms to make an enormous queue before

Jupiter to show him their babies.

Among them came the monkey, carrying her baby in her arms. It was a hairless, flat-nosed little thing, and when the gods saw it, they burst into laughter. However, the monkey hugged her baby and said, "Jupiter may give the prize to whoever he likes, but I shall always think my baby the most beautiful."

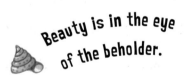

Beauty is in the eye of the beholder.

446

The Brother and Sister

Once upon a time, there lived a man who had two children, a boy and a girl. Everyone thought that the boy was very good-looking, but it was generally agreed that the girl was very plain. To save the boy from becoming big-headed and the girl from being miserable and jealous, the children's parents made sure that they never saw their own reflections.

However one day, they went to play in their mother's chamber, where their mother had forgotten to hide her mirror. The children saw their own features for the first time. The boy saw how handsome he was, and began to boast to his sister. But she was ready to cry at her plainness, and took this as an insult. She ran to her father to moan about her brother's vanity.

The man just laughed, and said, "Children, now you have seen yourselves, learn to make positive use of the glass. My boy, strive to be as good as it shows you to be handsome, and you, my girl, resolve to make up for the plainness of your features by the sweetness of your nature."

Good virtues are more important than beauty.

The Lion
and the
Hare

There was once a lion who was out hunting, prowling around the neighbourhood looking for tasty morsels to eat. He was delighted when he came across a sleeping hare. He was just about to snap her up in his jaws when he saw a passing stag out of the corner of his eye. The lion at once left the hare and went after the bigger prize.

The lion chased and chased the stag for as long as he had strength, but he could not overtake him. In the end he had to abandon the attempt. "Never mind," he said to himself, "I shall go back and gobble up the hare after all."

The lion bounded back to where he had previously seen the hare. However, she was nowhere to be seen. He had to go home without dinner after all, with his tail between his legs.

"It serves me right," he said, "I should have been content with what I had, instead of hankering after a better prize."

Don't let greed cause you to overreach yourself, or you could lose all.

The Cage-bird and the Bat

There was once a tiny bird that lived in a cage, which hung outside a window. The little captive longed for the skies she could see through the bars, and even though she no longer had the joy of flying, she sang with the most beautiful voice. She would have gladdened the hearts of all who heard her — except that she sang at night, when everyone was asleep.

One night, a bat came and clung to the bars of the cage, and asked the bird why she was silent by day and sang only at night.

"I have a very good reason for only singing at night," said the bird. "It was once when I was singing in the daytime that a bird-catcher was attracted by my voice, and he caught me. Since then I have only sung at night." But the bat replied, "It is no use doing that now, when you are a prisoner. If only you had done so before you were caught, you might still be free."

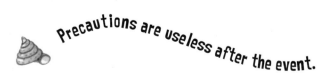

Precautions are useless after the event.

452

The Frogs
and the
Well

There were once two frogs who lived together in a marsh. It was damp and shady, with plenty of flies and worms to eat, just how they liked it. But one year the summer was very hot and dry. The marsh dried up, and the frogs were forced to leave and look for somewhere new to live.

They leapt and hopped for miles across the countryside, but all the ponds and lakes and streams and rivers were dried up like the marsh. The frogs had no option but to keep looking, for without water and shade they would dry up too.

Eventually they came to a deep well. One of them peered down into it — there was water at the bottom. The frog said to his friend, "This is the perfect place, let us jump in and settle here." But the other frog, who had a wiser head on his shoulders, replied, "Not so fast, my friend. Supposing this well dries up too, how should we get out again?"

Think twice before
you act.

The Crab and the Fox

There was once a crab who lived in a rock pool at the seashore. But he grew bored and restless, seeing the same surroundings all the time. He wanted a change of scenery, so he left the beach and went inland, scurrying sideways.

There, he found a meadow, which he thought looked beautiful – lush and green, and filled with flowers. He settled there, hoping it would be a good place to live.

But soon a hungry fox came along, and caught the crab. The fox had never seen a crab before and thought he smelled delicious! Just as he was going to be eaten up, the crab said, "This is what I deserve, for I had no business to leave my natural home by the sea and settle here as though I belonged to the land."

Be content with your lot.

The **Lion,** the **Fox** and the **Donkey**

There once lived a lion, a fox and a donkey, who agreed to help each other hunt for food. The unlikely partnership worked well, and they soon had a large amount of food.

Then the lion ordered the donkey to share out the spoils. The donkey did not particularly want the responsibility, but he dared not refuse. So he shared out the food as equally as he could, and humbly told the others they could choose before him which portion they wanted.

To the donkey's surprise, the lion gave a great

458

roar of rage, pounced, and devoured him. Then the lion turned to the fox and ordered him to try sharing out the spoils.

Trembling, the fox gathered the three piles of food into one big heap, then separated out just a tiny morsel for himself.

The lion snarled with satisfaction. "Who has taught you, my excellent fellow, the art of division?" he growled.

The fox replied, "I learnt it from the donkey, by witnessing his fate."

Happy are they who learn from the misfortunes of others.

The Two Pots

There **were once** two pots that had been left on the bank of a river. One was made of brass and the other of earthenware. As the tide rose, they both floated off down the stream. They were tossed this way and that way by the current, and the earthenware pot tried its best to keep away from the brass one. Then the brass one cried out, "Don't worry my friend, I will not hit you."

"But I may bash into you by accident," said the earthenware pot. "Whether I hit you, or you hit me, you'll be fine, but I will suffer for it."

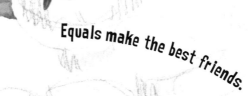

Equals make the best friends.

462

Narrow Escapes and Sticky Endings

The Swan
and the
Goose

There was once a rich man who wanted to show off to his neighbours. He went to market and bought a goose and a swan. He fed the goose well, making sure it grew plump, ready to be cooked for a feast one day. However, he planned to keep the swan, so he could hear its beautiful song from his window.

The time finally arrived for the man to hold his feast. His cook and kitchen assistants worked hard in preparation to make many delicious dishes. Then they had to kill the goose ready for cooking. So that night, the cook went out to catch it. He could hardly see his hand in front of his face, let alone tell one bird from the other. By mistake he caught the swan instead of the goose. The swan, knowing it was about to be killed, burst into one last beautiful song. The cook realized that he had the wrong bird – and so the swan was saved by its singing.

Sweet words may save us from danger, when harsh words fail.

The Frogs who Wanted a King

Once upon a time, there was a group of frogs who lived as happily as could be in a marshy swamp. Not many animals would enjoy the boggy conditions, but it suited the frogs.

Every day, they went splashing about through the puddles, without a care in the world. No one came near the slimy, grimy waters, so no one troubled them. But some of the frogs thought that this happy-go-lucky life was not right, that they should have a king and proper rules. So the frogs prayed to the great god Zeus, who ruled over the Earth, to give them what they wanted.

"Mighty Zeus," they cried, "please send us a king who will rule and keep us in order."

High up on Mount Olympus, where the gods and goddesses lived, Zeus laughed at the noisy croaking of the frogs.

'A king?' he thought. 'What would those silly creatures do with a king?' Instead, he threw down into the swamp a huge log, which landed with a SPLASH in the water.

The frogs were frightened out of their lives! They all rushed to the bank to see whatever had fallen from the sky. At first they thought it must be a horrible monster. But after a time, seeing that it did not move, one or two of the boldest frogs ventured out towards the log, and even dared to touch it. Still it did not move. Then the bravest of the frogs jumped upon the log and began dancing up and down on it. All the other frogs soon came and did the same. After that, they lost interest in the log. For some time they went about their business without taking any notice of the log lying in their midst.

But they still wanted a king. So they prayed to Zeus again, and said to him, "Please send us a king – not just a log, but a real king who will really rule over us."

This irritated Zeus. 'How ungrateful

and foolish they are,' he thought. So he sent a big stork that set to work gobbling up all the frogs. Then they wished they had never asked for a king in the first place, but it was too late.

Better no rule than cruel rule.

469

The Stag
and the
Hunter

One day, long ago, a stag came to drink at a pool in a wood. As he lapped at the cool, clear water, he admired his reflection.

"What a noble animal I am," he said to himself. "Which other animal has such noble horns as these, such handsome antlers!" But then the stag frowned. "Oh, but I wish my legs suited me better. They're so slim and slight compared to the rest of me. I wish they were more powerful."

At that moment, an arrow went whistling past his ear. The stag had been so engrossed in admiring himself that he had not noticed a hunter approaching. He bounded away at once, with the hunter in hot pursuit.

With the aid of his nimble legs, the stag got almost out of sight of the hunter. However, he wasn't looking properly where he was going. He plunged into some trees that had low-growing branches. Before the stag realized what was happening, his antlers were caught fast. As he struggled to get free, twisting this way and that, he just became more tangled. And of course, the hunter had time to catch up.

We often sneer at what is most useful to us.

The Workman and the Nightingale

It was a hot summer's night — so hot that a workman could not get to sleep. Instead, he lay with the window open, hoping that a little breeze might blow through, listening to the beautiful song of a nightingale. The little bird kept him company all night long, singing sweetly. The workman listened intently, and he was so delighted by its singing that he decided he had to have the bird for himself.

The next night, the workman set a trap for the nightingale and captured it. "Now that I have caught you," he cried, "you will always sing to me, whenever I want."

But the little bird held its chin high and proud and shook its head. "We nightingales never sing in a cage," it said.

"Then I will eat you," said the workman. "I have always heard that a nightingale on toast is a tasty snack."

The nightingale quivered in terror. "No, please don't eat me!" it begged. "Let me go free, and I will tell you three things that are worth far more than my little body."

The workman thought for a moment, but he didn't see how he could lose. "All right," he shrugged, and he set the bird free.

Without a moment's hesitation the nightingale flew up to the highest branch of a nearby tree and looked down at the workman, way out of reach below.

"The three things are pieces of advice," it trilled. "Firstly, never believe a captive's promise. Secondly, keep what you have. And thirdly, don't feel sad for what you have lost forever and cannot get back."

Then, while the workman was wondering how he could have been tricked by a tiny bird, the nightingale flew away.

Do not feel sorry about what is lost forever.

474

The **Young Thief**
and his
Mother

A **young man** had fallen in with bad friends. He had turned to a life of crime and stolen many things. But now he had finally been caught, and had been tried before a court and sentenced to prison. However, he asked to see his mother one last time — and his wish was granted.

When the thief's mother arrived, he said, "I want to whisper something to you." She brought her ear close to his mouth — and he bit it.

People nearby were horrified and demanded to know what he thought he was doing.

"It is to punish her," he said. "When I was young I began stealing little things, and brought them home to Mother. Instead of telling me off and punishing me, she laughed and said, 'It will not be noticed.' It is because of her that I am here today."

"He is right," said the judge. "Bring up a child in the right way, and when he is older, he will not go astray."

Teach a child well.

The Hare with many Friends

There was once a hare who was popular with the other animals. She was good-natured and fun to be with. Everyone claimed to be her friend. But one day she heard the sound of thundering hooves and baying hounds – huntsmen were approaching with sniffer dogs. The hare knew they were after her. What if she could not outrun them? She thought her friends might be able to help her escape instead.

So the hare ran off to see the horse, and asked him to carry her away from the hounds on his back. But he refused, stating that he had work to do for his master. "I'm sure," he said, "that the bull would be happy to help you."

So the hare dashed off to ask the bull, hoping that he would charge at the hounds with his horns. But the bull replied, "I am very sorry, but I have an appointment. However I feel sure that the goat will do as you ask."

The hare sped off to see the goat. However, he feared that his back might be too bumpy for the hare. "I don't want to hurt you," he explained. "Why don't you ask the ram? His back is woolly and soft."

So the hare hurried to see the ram and told him about the hunters. The ram replied, "My friend, I do not like to interfere, as hounds have been known to eat sheep as well as hares."

The hare was growing desperate. The sound of the hunt was getting ever closer. She sprinted off to see the calf, as a very last hope. However, the calf said that he too was unable to help. He did not like to take the responsibility, as so many adults had declined the task.

By this time the hounds were very near. There was nothing left for the hare to do but run for her life — and luckily, she escaped.

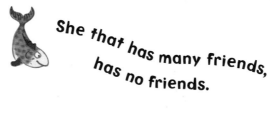

She that has many friends, has no friends.

The **Two Fellows**
and the **Bear**

Once upon a time, two men were travelling through a wood together, chatting about this and that to pass the time. All at once, a huge, bear rushed out at them.

The travellers were of course terrified. One ran for his life. He dashed into a thicket of trees, seized hold of the low-hanging

branches and gathered them around him to hide himself. The other traveller threw himself to the ground, face-down in the dust. He kept still, not even daring to breathe. The bear came up to him, sniffing him all over. But at last with a growl it slouched off. It thought the man must be dead, and bears do not like dead meat.

Then, when the man in the trees saw that the bear had gone, he came out and returned to his travelling companion. Laughing, he said, "What was it that the bear whispered to you?"

"It told me," said the other, "a friend who runs off and leaves you at the first sign of trouble should not be trusted."

Never trust a friend who deserts you at a pinch.

The Trumpeter taken Prisoner

Once, during a time of war, there was a brave army trumpeter who went too close to the enemy on the battlefield. Enemy soldiers captured him and dragged him back behind their lines, delighted that he could no longer sound out the other side's orders. The soldiers were about to put him to death, when the young trumpeter begged for mercy.

"Look at me – I am not a fighter," he said. "I don't even carry a weapon. All I do is blow this trumpet – and how can that hurt you? So I ask you, why do you want to kill me? Please spare my life, I have done nothing to you."

But the enemy soldiers answered grimly, "You may not have had a hand in the fighting against us, but by sounding out the orders, you guide and encourage your soldiers in battle. They and you have killed hundreds of our men, so now you must pay the price for your music."

Those who stir up trouble are as guilty as those who carry it out.

The Bat and the Weasels

A **bat once lived** with his fellow bats in a deep, dark cave. They lived happily, flying out to hunt at night and returning to sleep during the day. However one evening, the bat flew into a tree and fell to the ground. Unfortunately, a weasel sniffed him out. Before the bat could fly away, the weasel had pounced and caught him.

The bat begged to be let go. The weasel said he couldn't do that because he was an enemy of birds. "I'm not a bird, I'm a mouse," said the bat.

The weasel looked at the bat. "So you are," he said, "now I look at you," and he let the bat go.

Soon after, the bat was caught in the same way by another weasel, and begged for his life.

"No," said the weasel, "I never let a mouse go."

"I'm not a mouse," said the bat, "I'm a bird."

The weasel examined the bat. "So you are," he said, and he too let the bat go.

Look and see which way the wind blows before you commit yourself.

The Apes and the Two Travellers

Once upon a time, two men were travelling on a journey together. One of the men always spoke the truth, but the other never said anything but lies.

After some time, they came to a land of apes. The travellers were very surprised when a band of apes seized them, and dragged them off to see their king. The King Ape had demanded that they be captured because he wanted to know what humans said about him and his subjects.

The travellers were taken into the king's

throne room. The king had commanded that all the apes be present to hear what humans said about them. The king sat on a throne – because that was what human kings did – and arranged his subjects in rows.

When the men were dragged in, the king asked, "What sort of a king do I seem to be to you, O strangers?"

The lying traveller replied, "You seem to me a most mighty king."

"And what is your opinion of those you see around me?" the King Ape asked.

"These," the lying traveller answered, "are worthy companions of yours, fit at least to be ambassadors and leaders of armies."

The ape and all his court were pleased with the lies. They commanded that a handsome present be given to the flatterer. On this, the truthful traveller thought to himself, 'If so great a reward be given for a lie, how may I be treated, if, according to my custom, I tell the truth?'

The King Ape turned to the truthful traveller. "And how do I and my friends seem to you?" he demanded.

"You are," the truthful traveller answered, "a most excellent ape. And all of your companions, who are copying you, are all excellent apes too."

The King Ape, enraged at this, threw the traveller to his furious fellow apes.

Don't always assume that the values of others match your own.

The Flea and the Man

There was once a tiny flea that bit a man again and again — it would not give up. The man suffered it for a long time, but finally he could take no more. He looked everywhere on himself until he found the flea and at last succeeded in catching it. Holding it between his finger and thumb, he said, "Who are you, wretched little creature, that you

dare to cause me such misery?"

Now the flea was not so bold. It whimpered in a weak little voice, "Oh, sir! I beg of you, let me go, don't kill me! I am such a little thing that I can't do you much harm."

But the man said, "I am going to kill you at once. Whatever is bad has got to be destroyed. It doesn't matter how little harm it may cause."

Do not waste your pity on a scamp.

The Stag
in the
Ox-stall

There **was once a stag** who lived in a
forest. His home was in some high crags
amongst the trees, where he felt quite safe. But
one day, to his horror, he heard hounds
approaching. He was forced to flee, as the
hounds chased him through the forest and out
towards a nearby village.

The desperate stag galloped into a farmyard
and dashed into a stable where a number of
oxen were gathered. He looked around in terror
for a hiding place, and in the end buried himself

under a pile of hay in an empty stall. He lay there, as still and silent as he could, hidden except for the very tips of his antlers.

After a few minutes, one of the oxen looked at the heap of hay and said, "Whatever made you come in here? The huntsmen who are after you may not find you, but you are running the risk of being captured by the village cattle herders."

Then the stag replied, "Please, let me stay for now. When night comes I shall easily escape under cover of darkness."

So the oxen went back to minding their own business and left the stag to his hiding.

That afternoon, several farm-hands came to tend the oxen, but none noticed the stag. He began to relax, congratulating himself on his escape, and he thanked the oxen for letting him stay.

"We wish you well," said one oxen, "but you are not out of danger yet. If the master comes, you will certainly be found, for nothing ever escapes his keen eyes."

Sure enough, in came the master and made a great to-do about the way the oxen were kept. "The beasts are starving," he cried, "here, give them more hay." As he spoke, he seized an armful himself from the pile where the stag lay hidden, and at once found him. Calling his men, he caught and killed the stag, ready for eating.

There is no eye like the master's.

The **Tunny-fish**
and the
Dolphin

Once upon a time in the ocean, far out in deep water, a dolphin was chasing a tunny-fish. They both splashed through the water at a great rate, swimming with all their might, and gradually the dolphin began gaining on the tunny-fish.

Just as the dolphin was about to seize him, the tunny-fish gave a huge leap that carried him right out of the water and onto a sandbank. In the heat of the chase the dolphin followed him, and there they both lay out of the water,

gasping for dear life. When the
tunny-fish saw that his enemy
was doomed like himself,
he said, "I don't mind
having to die now, for I
see that the cause of
my death is about to
share the same fate."

If you seek to harm someone, they will get great
satisfaction in seeing you come to harm too.

The Dog
and the
Cook

A **rich man once decided** to throw a party for all his family and friends. The man's dog thought it would be a good opportunity to invite one of his friends too, so he went to another dog and said, "My master is giving a feast – there'll be a fine spread, so come and dine with me tonight."

The friend was excited to be asked. He came along at the appointed time and, when he saw the preparations being made in the kitchen he said to himself, "I'm in luck. I'll take care to eat enough tonight to last me two or three days." At the same time he wagged his tail, by way of showing the master's dog how delighted he was.

But just then the cook caught sight of him. She was furious to see a strange dog in the kitchen. In her annoyance, she picked him up and threw him out of the window.

The poor dog limped away, howling dismally. Soon, some other dogs met him, and said, "Well, what sort of a dinner did you get?" to which he replied, "I had a splendid time. The wine was so good, and I drank so much of it, that I don't remember how I got out of the house!"

Be wary of favours done at the expense of others.

The Boy Bathing

There was once a boy who fancied bathing in the river, as it was a hot day and the water looked so fresh and cool. He wasn't a very good swimmer, but he made up his mind not to let that put him off. He stripped off his clothes and carefully stepped a little way into the river.

It felt wonderful. A little bolder, he bent down until his shoulders were underneath the surface. Ah, now he was much cooler! The boy was getting braver with every minute. He began jumping about, splashing – until suddenly the bottom dropped away from him and his feet could no longer touch the floor.

Then the boy began kicking and thrashing, trying to save himself, although he made no progress towards the bank. He was right out of his depth and in danger of drowning.

Fortunately, a man who was passing heard his cries for help. He went to the riverside and began to scold him for being so careless as to get into deep water – however, he made no attempt to help him. "Oh, sir," cried the boy, "please help me first and tell me off afterwards."

Give assistance, not advice, in a crisis.

The
Bee-Keeper

There was once a bee-keeper who had
many hives full of honey. A thief had his
eye on them and was determined to steal the
honey for himself. He waited until the bee-keeper
went out one day, then broke in and stole every
last morsel from the hives.

When the bee-keeper returned and found
the hives empty, he was very upset. It wasn't
long before the bees came back from gathering
nectar and, finding their hives overturned and
the keeper standing by, they thought it was he

who had taken all their honey. In their rage, they stung the bee-keeper, swarming over him. At this the bee-keeper was furious and cried, "You ungrateful scoundrels, you let the thief who stole my honey get away with it and then you sting me, the person who has always taken such care of you!"

If you hit back, make sure you have the right person.

The Dog, the Rooster and the Fox

A dog and a rooster became great friends, and agreed to travel on a journey together. They set out early in the morning, travelled all day, and at dusk began looking for a place to stay for the night. They found a tree that looked like a suitable place for them both. The rooster flew up into the branches, while the dog curled himself up inside the trunk, which was hollow.

At the break of day the rooster woke up and began to crow as usual. A fox heard this, and wishing to make a breakfast of the rooster, came and stood under the tree and begged him to come down.

"I should like," said the fox, "to get to know one who has such a beautiful voice."

The rooster wasn't fooled for one minute. He thought very quickly and replied, "Would you just wake my butler who sleeps at the foot of the tree? He'll open the door and let you in." The fox accordingly rapped on the trunk, and out rushed the dog, who tore him into pieces.

Do not be taken in by flattery.

The Wolf and his Shadow

There was once a big, hairy wolf, who was roaming across a plain at the end of a day's hunting. The sun was low in the sky, and the wolf noticed that his shadow was enormous.

"I knew I was big, but I didn't realize I was that big!" said the wolf to himself. "Why, I am a very fine creature indeed. Everyone should be afraid of me — and I should be afraid of no one. Fancy me bowing down to a lion! I ought to be King of the Beasts." Not caring about any danger, the wolf began strutting along as if he was the finest animal on Earth. But just then a lion pounced upon him, seized him in his jaws, and began to eat him. "Alas," the wolf cried, "had I not lost sight of the facts, I shouldn't have been ruined by my fancies."

Be realistic about your own potential.

505

The Lion, the Fox and the Stag

There was once a lion who had become very ill. He lay in his den, barely able to move, and starving hungry for he could not go out to hunt. One day, his friend the fox came to pay him a visit, to see how he was. The desperate lion asked for some help.

"My good friend," he said, "I wish you would go to the nearby wood and trick

506

the big stag who lives there to come to my den. I am craving some tasty stag for my dinner."

The fox was happy to help. So he went to the wood and found the stag, and said to him, "My dear sir, you're in luck. You know the lion, our king, well, he's at the point of death, and has appointed you his successor to rule over the beasts. I hope you won't forget that I was the first to bring you the news. And now I must go back to him, and if you take my advice, you'll come too and be with him in his last moments."

The stag was highly flattered at the thought of the lion choosing him to be the next king. Delighted, he followed the fox to the lion's den, suspecting nothing. No sooner had he got inside than the lion sprang upon him. However, he was weak from lack of food and misjudged his attack. The stag got away with only his ears torn.

The lion was dreadfully disappointed, for he was so hungry that it felt as if his tummy was on fire. So he begged the fox to have another try at coaxing the stag to his den.

"It'll be almost impossible this time," said the fox, "but I'll try." And off he went to the wood a second time.

The fox found the stag resting, recovering from his fright. When he saw the fox he cried, "You scoundrel, what do you mean by trying to lure me to my death like that? I suggest you go now, or I'll kill you with my antlers."

But the fox was entirely shameless. "What a coward you are," he said, "surely you didn't think the lion meant any harm? Why, he was only going to whisper some royal secrets into your ear when you went off like a scared rabbit. You have rather disgusted him, and I think he might make the wolf king instead, unless you come back and show you have some spirit. I promise he won't hurt you, and I will be your faithful servant."

At that, the stag was foolish enough to return. This time the lion made no mistake, but overpowered him, and enjoyed a delicious dinner. The fox, meanwhile, watched for his chance, and when the lion wasn't looking, stole the stag's brains as a reward for his trouble. Presently the lion began searching for them, and the fox said, "I don't think there's much point in looking for the brains — a creature who twice walked into a lion's den can't have had any."

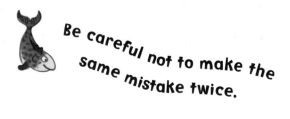

Be careful not to make the same mistake twice.

The Farmer, his Boy and the Rooks

A **farmer once sowed** a field of wheat. He kept watch over it, for lots of rooks kept settling and eating the grain. With him went his boy, carrying a slingshot, so the farmer could scare the birds away. But whenever the farmer asked for the slingshot the birds understood what he said, and they were off in a moment.

"My lad," said the

farmer, "we must get the better of these birds. From now on, when I want the slingshot, I'll just say 'Humph!' and you must pass it to me quickly."

The flock soon came back. "Humph!" said the farmer. Of course, the birds took no notice, but the boy handed the farmer the slingshot, and he had time to fire several stones among them before they got away.

As the birds escaped they met some cranes, who asked them what the matter was. "It's those men!" said one rook. "They say one thing and mean another, which has just been the death of some of our friends."

Beware of people who say one thing but mean another.

About the Artists

 Frank Endersby has always loved painting and drawing. His favourite medium is watercolour and he brings his own interpretation to stories, especially when there is lots of action and characters to stretch his imagination.

 Marco Furlotti used to be a chemist, but for the last two years he has worked as a children's illustrator and author. His passion for drawing and storytelling is clearly expressed in his illustrations, which are full of energy and humour. Marco lives in the beautiful countryside surrounding the historic city of Parma, Italy.

 Natalie Hinrichsen works in her loft studio in a suburb of Cape Town, South Africa. She likes illustrating folk stories in gouache and watercolour. Natalie has been illustrating children's books since 1996, and in 2005 she won the Vivian Wilkes award for illustration.

 Tamsin Hinrichsen works in Cape Town, South Africa with her twin sister, Natalie. After studying graphic design, she decided to be a children's book illustrator. She likes the bright colours and dry brush texture of acrylics and particularly enjoys illustrating animal stories. Natalie has illustrated several books in South Africa as well as internationally.

 Jan Lewis is based in Oxfordshire, UK, and has been working as an illustrator since 1978. She has produced work for many British publishers, and BBC children's television. Jan recently gained an MA in Authorial Illustration and now enjoys writing and illustrating her own books for children.

Marcin Piwowarski has been painting from a very young age, and now specializes in children's illustration. His style is energetic, with strong brushstrokes and depth of colour. Marcin's work has been published in the UK, Norway and the USA.